MAŠA KOLANOVIĆ
UNDERGROUND BARBIE

COPYRIGHT © 2025 Maša Kolanović
TRANSLATION COPYRIGHT © 2025 Ena Selimović
DESIGN & LAYOUT Nikša Eršek
PUBLISHED BY Sandorf Passage
South Portland, Maine, United States
IMPRINT OF Sandorf
Severinska 30, Zagreb, Croatia
sandorfpassage.org
Printed in the United States of America
2nd printing, 2025

Sandorf Passage books are available to the
trade through Independent Publishers Group:
ipgbook.com | (800) 888-4741.

Library of Congress Control Number: 2024940225

ISBN: 978-9-53351-512-0

Also available as an ebook;
ISBN: 978-9-53351-514-4

This book is published with financial support by the
Republic of Croatia's Ministry of Culture and Media.

Republika
Hrvatska
Ministarstvo
kulture
i medija
Republic
of Croatia
Ministry
of Culture
and Media

MAŠA KOLANOVIĆ
UNDERGROUND BARBIE

translated from croatian by ENA SELIMOVIĆ

SAN-
DORF
PAS-
SAGE

SOUTH PORTLAND | MAINE

for my grandma Roža, with love

Wartime Necessities

UNTIL THAT DAY I thought you could only hear such a sound at an air show, when the planes in the sky left blue, white, and red trails and the pilots performed breakneck stunts like Tom Cruise in *Top Gun*. Except on this particular day, all the Tom Cruises were wearing the olive-green uniform of the Yugoslav People's Army.

I'd never been to an air show, but in the sixth grade my brother enrolled in a plane-modeling class, and their comrade took them to one as a reward. Then suddenly the air shows ceased, just like we were no longer allowed to call our teachers "Comrade!" Everything was repackaged. Including the word "comrade," which was folded into "Mister" and "Miss." And while we'd lavishly been inducted into the Yugoslav Union of Pioneers, there was no pomp or circumstance when the time came for the upgrade in rank to the League of Socialist Youth. At school, Tito's portrait was replaced by the

Croatian coat of arms and the crucifix. Mass was no longer held in a two-bedroom apartment off Bolšić Street but in our school lobby. Our school was no longer named Branko Ćopić Elementary after the Yugoslav writer but "Island Elementary," and we no longer went on field trips to the Yugoslav Pioneer City but to an ancient Croatian castle or some such thing up north. Most of my friends with newly out-of-fashion names—Saša, Bojan, and Boro—moved away overnight.

would have been a reckless gamble, and Barbie was merely one share of my wartime necessities. I mean, what was Barbie without her abundance of flawless belongings? She would be reduced to the plainest peasant girl from the Handicrafts store, and I had seen more than enough of those before the day arrived when *She* finally knocked on my door (to be precise, my mailbox). But that was long ago, long before all that business with the planes and the sirens. In the beginning, my mother had absolutely refused to buy me that sliver of plastic perfection, but she was talked about, she was known, and some, like one Ana F. from building #17, had even acquired her before I had. Everyone from our building had watched Her. Even though she was so small, oh, that platinum-blonde cowgirl was clearly visible in Ana's hands. And not just *visible*. On the raised sewage vent where the girls from #17 played, you could just *feel* there was something extraordinary present, something that must have fallen from the sky. Ana's aunt had sent her this real Barbie by airmail from America. The blonde who could bend her knees and came with a ton of accessories. Rumor had it that the folk singer Neda Ukraden's niece owned as many as fifty! Jealousy is not the right word to express the feelings that overcame those of us who didn't have a real Barbie. Yes, a real one. For the record, there was no shortage of wannabe Barbies made from abysmal varieties of plastic. Non-Mattel fakes with puffy cheeks, unbendable knees, poorly sewn clothes, and catastrophic shoes, who weren't even called Barbie, but Stefi, Barbara, Cyndy—a whole gamut of stupid names. Needless to say, not having a real Barbie meant being profoundly unhappy. My uncle Ivo from New York finally put an end to this dark Before Barbie Era and sent one to our home, because, unlike all the others, he simply couldn't let his niece in Yugoslavia be deprived of that small but important token of prestige and prosperity.

It was the dawn of a new day when she arrived in our mailbox, which my mother and I opened together. At least in that moment, despite her previous show of disinterest, my mother caught Barbie fever. I saw it in her eyes. And it honestly didn't make me think she was any less in charge, since you would have to be blind (at the bare minimum) to remain indifferent in Barbie's presence. This fever was marked by the realization that only a thin layer of brown wrapping paper stood between me and my most coveted piece of plastic, preventing me from even guessing which one would be my first Barbie—no less, my first *real* one. When I unwrapped the package, it simply couldn't have come out more perfectly, because my first Barbie was also my favorite TV character: Krystle Carrington from *Dynasty*! (On second thought, it might not have actually been that Krystle, since the box had "Crystal" written on it, but this detail was immaterial

MAŠA KOLANOVIĆ

and I imagined it was Krystle in the flesh.) And when I opened the box and loosened Crystal Barbie from her protective restraints, it felt like I had come into physical contact with a deity. Only *this* deity was much more glorious than all those fat and clumsy prehistoric goddesses that had set my corneas ablaze, given my exposure to all sorts of exhibits at the Archaeological Museum

my mom and dad hauled me through in the hope that I would acquire a "cultural sense" from a very young age. Oh, that shimmery little pink ribbon tied around her iridescent, waist-defined cocktail dress, with a matching shimmery pink at her neckline; her small ring; her earrings; her little silver sequined shoes; her hairbrush and comb; the scent of fresh plastic—it was all so real! She was no longer an unattainable object in commercials on the satellite channels, inviting me to imagine for the umpteenth time that I was playing with her as if she were really mine. For the first time in my life, I had something that was truly valuable.

My next Barbie was gifted by my uncle Marko. Although the matter at hand now concerned my *second* Barbie and the first would always be first, my second Barbie was really something miraculous. It was only when Uncle Marko brought her, Day-to-Night Barbie, that I began to recognize Barbie's true potential and how many additional little things could accompany one single Barbie. During the day, Day-to-Night Barbie wore her velvety pink suit jacket and skirt, accessorized with a computer, a hat, a briefcase, and a pair of pumps. On the box she was pictured deeply engrossed in her work and handling some bills, but at one and the same time, above the tasteful prescription glasses that made her look smarter, she was throwing secret glances at Ken. Oh, the romantic convolutions that took place between them in that little office overlooking the Twin Towers! In the evening, that selfsame Barbie would slip out of her suit jacket to uncover a shimmery pink bodice; she'd turn her plush skirt inside out to unveil a sequin trim, then put on her open-toed heels, grab her clutch, and head out with Ken to some super-expensive restaurant in Manhattan. Was there anything more perfect than this Barbie? I spent hours upon hours admiring her ability to effortlessly transform from businesswoman to vamp, vamp to businesswoman. The third, Tropical Barbie, was given to me by my uncle Lolo. Her accessories were rather modest, but you had to admit she possessed qualities neither my first nor my second Barbie possessed. Sure, my cousin Karolina from New York had ten Tropicals lying idle in her overseas suitcase, which she habitually left strewn all over Grandma Luca's house in Privlaka, but against the earthy gray landscape of Sloboština, my Tropical girl was absolutely singular. She had

MAŠA KOLANOVIĆ

long blonde hair (all the way to her knees), a little Hawaiian swimsuit, and a skirt (imitation flowers). She wasn't a glam heroine from *Dynasty*, she wasn't a businesswoman from Manhattan, she was a beauty of nature—the ocean, the sun, and the waves. Even though that wretched, barefoot soul had only a single hairbrush to her name, Tropical Barbie was unsurpassed as far as her natural attributes were concerned.

From that point, their numbers grew in an orderly fashion. The fourth in my collection was not a Barbie but an Aerobic Skipper—Barbie's little sister or cousin, whichever you imagined. My parents bought her for me when they went to Rome with my brother, aunt, and cousin. I say "bought," but they essentially bought me *off* with the Skipper because there was no room for me in our Renault 4. But hey, being bought off with a Skipper wasn't all that bad. Aerobic Skipper was almost equally perfect—like Barbie, but of a lower class. They'd initially intended to buy me some pitiful tennis player who only came with a crummy little racket, but since they subsequently decided to stay in Rome a week longer, the gift had to reflect those changes with a significant upgrade. Although Skipper could never be Barbie, because she had smaller boobs and it was anatomically impossible for her to wear heels, anyone with an ounce of dignity had to have at least one Skipper. Obviously, along with a Ken, who was absolutely indispensable, despite the fact that no grander euphoria could be obtained from owning a Ken, given that he merely served as another one of Barbie's accessories. The heart of the matter is, I'd only seen Aerobic Skipper in the Barbie catalog that I was given free of charge in the American pavilion at the Zagreb Fair and kept in a special folder to protect it from accidental damage. She came with every possible piece of sporting equipment imaginable, from a pair of leggings, some leg warmers, a leotard, and two pairs of sneakers (pink and yellow) to visors, tennis skirts, and tracksuits. But dwelling on excess in Barbie World was itself excessive, because no one—*no one*—in this world could have an excess of anything from Barbie World. A shortage—yes! A shortage always. Just how much was missing from as modest a Barbie household as mine? Listing the items would take a lifetime—and longer, if you named every single accessory down to the tiniest one, all the pinks and purples on those catalog pages I had spent so many hours staring at in the hope of bringing them to life, in the hope that those pictures would become real, objects I could have and hold.

Ah, those images of Barbie World in those Barbie magazines that turned my longing into immeasurable sorrow. The commercials between segments of *Fun Factory* that I watched on Sky via satellite. And to think that one Saturday morning, in the very middle of an episode of *Fun Factory*, my mom and dad had dragged me to a "Passion of the Christ" exhibit where there were hundreds of different crucifixes on display. In that moment, all I wanted, more than anything else in my life, was to set my eyes on the endless combinations of Barbie outfits that the commercials advertised to the beat of *"Fun, fun, fun!"* Eventually, night would ease my suffering, but every fresh glimpse into that perfect world, elaborated to its teensy and even teensier details, dared to crush my body, in danger of bursting from all those intense longings.

And yet, little by little, you come to terms with your deprivation and begin seeking out other solutions. They were certainly not lacking in my Barbie household, scrapped together as it was with every "other solution" under the sun. Being deprived of the catalog's offerings had so twisted my mind that I could associate absolutely anything on planet Earth with Barbie: the washbasin my grandmother used to soak her feet in scented salt became a pool for Barbie; cassette holders sitting upright served perfectly as armchairs for Barbie; bricks from the balcony, along with some soil from my mother's potted plants, functioned as building materials for Barbie hanging gardens; the eraser caps from my mechanical pencils were an adequate set of glasses for Barbie and her friends; perfume samples became top-shelf bottles of whiskey for the cocktail parties Barbie threw (and not so rarely,

either); a red Converse All Star transformed into a red Ferrari (one-seater); hand towels were rolled into little beds; aluminum cans lined up together formed a promotional bar for Barbie. The motto of my personal Barbie design was: "Name anything in the world, and I'll tell you what it can become for Barbie!" Many of the things I made myself with the help of other forced laborers—like my grandmother, who upholstered cardboard armchairs with the purple linen of her old slips, while my mother sewed pillows for them. And unlike the wretched boys' clothes they sewed for me, my mother and grandmother were perfectly capable of designing sexy-flexy outfits when it came to dressing Barbie. Needless to say, the little outfits they made could never measure up to the originals, but there were some truly brilliant ready-made creations. Of the utmost importance was finding the right fabric—e.g., an old swimsuit made from colorful synthetic material or a curtain that resembled undergarments. The best example in the latter category was, unquestionably, the transparent corset my mother sewed according to a picture in the Barbie catalog. Barbie in that little corset and lying on a bed beside a small nightstand on which she could lay a fake book (she would never read it anyway) next to Ken's picture (a cutout of Ken's head glued to a scrap of cardboard)—it was almost a perfect copy of the original scene.

My first genuine pieces of Barbie furniture arrived somewhat later. Closest to genuine, that is. Although Cyndy herself could never be mistaken for Barbie, her furniture, at least, allowed her to act the part. The furniture for Cyndy was cheaper than the furniture for Barbie, so my mother bought me the furniture for Cyndy. First, just a small vanity table with a battery-powered lamp that actually turned on, and then a bed as well. A pink bed with a gold (imitation) vertical-bar headboard. Once, my brother's friends used miniature handcuffs from a Kinder egg to shackle poor Barbie to that headboard and appointed Ken to do all kinds of abominable things to her. Speaking of Ken, he joined my little Barbie household completely unexpectedly. He came in a bundle package with a brunette wannabe Barbie and two children—all sharing the name of Sweetheart Family. Worse, both of the adults wore engraved wedding rings. I'd only asked my grandmother for a Ken, but Grandma had to go and get me this little holy family set that neither I nor any of my Barbies received with a warm welcome, even though Barbie was by Mattel's nature an actual sweetheart. That slipper-wearing sissy of a husband was all but

glued to his brunette Sweetheart spouse and those two children she had borne for him. They even wore these stupid little matching aprons for the children's bath time, making an intervention into that humdrum idyll all but necessary. And whenever a blonde Barbie tried to woo Ken, that engraved wedding ring stuck out like a sore thumb. Oh, why couldn't it have been a removable ring? My grandmother had committed a grave disservice by picking out this set. Now, every relationship between Ken and the blonde Barbies automatically constituted an adultery. What followed this fundamentally unfortunate family was another Skipper—from a duty-free shop in Zadar. I managed to convince my uncle Marko that she was indispensable. She came dressed in a swimsuit that changed colors according to the water temperature. Although the most wondrous bluish color would sweep over her tiny frozen suit, basking in the springs of the so-called mountain-basin sink was not exactly Skipper's preferred method of relaxation.

In sum: three Barbies, two Skippers, the adulterous hubby Ken with the brunette Barbie, their two children, a plethora of sewn clothes alongside a handful of genuine pieces, one vanity table, and one bed. That was the full inventory of my initial assets I needed to protect somehow, to secure in the event of a catastrophe, since no personal liability insurance could possibly compensate me were Sloboština to be struck by surface-to-air or air-to-surface missiles, cluster bomblets, machine guns, automatic rifles, assault rifles, bombs, or poison gas. Hence why everything needed to be crammed into my small suitcase. And not simply crammed, but conserved, embalmed in a way against all the dust and shrapnel that might fall upon not only them, but upon all of us. First, each Barbie was individually placed into a plastic bag (the ones my mother used for freezing meat, fish, fruits, and vegetables), then individually wrapped in a towel before then reuniting with all the other Barbies and wannabes in a special canvas bag that was only then stowed in the suitcase. The clothes were stored in a separate baggie, along with a few scented mothballs I stole from my mother's drawer, and the vanity table was disassembled and returned to its original box. The only problem was the little bed: no amount of mastery in packing could make it conform to the confines of my suitcase. I stormed my brain trying to figure out how best to pack and preserve it, how best to transport this small and exceptionally valuable relic to the catacombs. But, after a lengthy brainstorm and an attempt at compressing the contents of the whole case, the situation with the bed remained unresolved. As a matter of fact, its unresolved status offered a faint glimmer of hope that nothing terrible would actually happen, that no siren or war would come to pass. But they did. The bed situation was resolved ad hoc.

We had to get going to the basement *this instant*; all the neighbors were already flying down the stairs, and my mother and father were rushing us. As I sprinted toward our apartment door with my suitcase in hand and the little pink bed with its golden frame under my arm, I heard a clap and felt the hot embers on my face. It was a slap from my brother, and the words "Leave that bed, retard!" It was neither the time nor the place for arguing, so I was forced to comply. The little bed was left at the mercy of the Yugoslav National Army. Come what may! We headed down the stairs, and I grew terrified of the planes and of everything that had begun to unfold. The planes continued to hiss past, a little more then, and since I could no longer see them, only hear them, I imagined them as pictures in *The Illustrated History of Aviation*, in a section called "Warriors of the Sky."

When we reached the basement, the whole building was already there: Tea, and Dea, and Svjetlana, and Ana P., and Ana Matić, and Borna, and Krešo, and Sanjica, and Marina. Everyone had already landed. I remember that I couldn't stop crying, and then, after half an hour, the siren stopped and we all headed back to our homes.

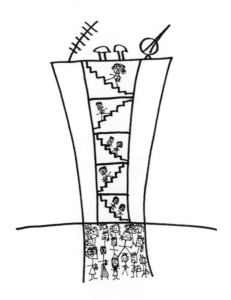

That night I slept in my mother and father's bed. "Slept"? More like: listened intently in case I happened to hear the "steel wings of our army." And as I finally sank into sleep, Pilot Barbie flew over my thoughts in a pink camouflage suit, streaking the sky a glaring pink in an episode of *Fear Factory*. Because Barbie could be anything—*anything*—she wanted. Way more than the catalogs and commercials led you to believe.

MAŠA KOLANOVIĆ

The Last Twin Peaks

IN THE DARKNESS of the room, two figurines were firmly pressed against each other. A blackout had gone into effect. All the blinds were drawn in the apartment and only faint candlelight was permitted, else the voices of middle-aged misters instantly echoed through the amphitheater formed by Sloboština's buildings: "Turn off the light!" or "Turn off the light, goddamn it!" in place of, say, a feature of peacetime like "Come get your potaaatoes! Who wants to buy some potaaaatoes? Potaaatoes!" The little park behind our building and the area surrounding it were pitch-black. All the orange-headed streetlights—which in long summer nights attracted a swarming motley crew of bugs, and which we'd carve our names and grade level on, or tie our jump rope around (if we were missing the obligatory third player for gumi-gumi), and which sent many of us homeward when they came on—all of them went dead in those moments, which were nowhere near as luminous as Barbie's wedding dress. So, I was in my room, sitting on the floor in darkness, my back resting against my bed and my feet like pliers, clutching Tropical Barbie and Sweetheart Family Ken in a rigid embrace, while with both hands I held a flashlight pointed at the pinkie finger to which I'd strung a disco ball (sized for a decoration pine tree). The disco ball's countless colorful glass pieces lit up the room, scanning the shelf of non-Barbie toys and the posters of Michael Jackson cuddling a tiger cub and Patrick Swayze wearing the uniform of a Confederate soldier in the American Civil War. The light penetrated their evening intimacy like a small raid by rainbow. Without a single ounce of coquettish delay, Tropical Barbie plunged her delicate and frightened self into the hold of Ken's broad shoulders and enticing stack of plastic (but rock-hard) abs as the radio blared "Zadnja ruža Hrvatska" (The Last Rose Croatia) by Prljavo kazalište.

Ru u u u u Žo! Moja ru-ži-ce e e,
Sve sam suze isplakO, noću zbog te-be-e e ...

Ro-o-ooose-oh! My little ro-o-ose,
All the te-ears I shed, at ni-ight in your stead ...

MAŠA KOLANOVIĆ

went the song, lagging slightly behind the rotations per second of the colorful squares. Beside this rather pitiful disco podium stood my ever-ready suitcase. After that first siren, the following day there was another, and then another, and then school was closed until further notice, but all I managed to do during those two days was pack and unpack the Barbies and play on my own (without even furnishing the apartment)—and in a fairly agitated state no less, because every so often we had to head back down to the basement. The entire Barbie World, in those precautionary early days of the war, was reduced to playing with naked bodies that did nothing but slow dance, sleep, and skip around the room like angels with amputated wings, wending their way from an imaginary house to an imaginary beachside bar, and vice versa. I, in the meantime, and in place of the Tropics, migrated multiple times daily from my room to the basement, and vice versa. As the Barbies' small, periodically spotlit silhouettes continued swinging left and right to the rhythm of the song, my brother's room radiated the sound of his Zorro video game, along with the blue flashes of the television screen our Commodore 64 was hooked up to and the steady curses my brother directed at the TV, given the recurring appearance of a line that split the screen, thereby making it hard to guide Zorro and collect points at each level of the Mexican underground. That undesirable horizon, right in the middle of the screen, drove us insane. There wasn't a thing we didn't try to make it disappear. Smacking the television around yielded the best results, but this wasn't exactly an approach you could adopt in perpetuity. On one occasion, we even made the sign of the cross over the screen by sprinkling holy water from a little plastic bottle with the image of Saint Marija Bistrička. But the line kept unveiling itself, and always the moment Avenger Zorro began to excel, against all odds, in his fight to overpower the gangs. As my brother fought the hard fight in Mexico, from the living room you could see, like so many distant explosions, flashes coming from the big television our mom and dad were watching. Not a single shred of news or segment of informational programming was to be missed, so my brother and I abandoned even the idea of protesting to watch a film on Sky. We each withdrew into our own chambers and waited for the powerwielders to grow bored of sitting through the one thousand and one political commentaries on the HTV channel.

And then suddenly, as though under a spell, we were gathered round by a sound gloomier than "The Last Rose Croatia" or any other slow song ever written. From the television in the living room, like a siren, the theme song of *Twin Peaks* drew us

MAŠA KOLANOVIĆ

together on the couch, and to top it off, it was the season finale we'd all been eagerly anticipating, though you could undoubtedly flip to any other channel and find local breaking news with far more tense content. But that was out of the question now,

because on this particular night, in this last episode of *Twin Peaks*, it would finally be revealed who had brutally murdered Laura Palmer, the beautiful high school girl from a small town in Washington State, and left her corpse, wrapped in plastic like supermarket chicken, by a giant log. Although the state of domestic affairs had become exceptionally grave and every new piece of information changed the course and outcome of events, not finding out the truth about Laura Palmer's murder under such utterly mysterious circumstances was almost a matter of life and death. We each boarded the couch and sailed off from our own country to a distant American hinterland. The television emitted rays of light, while the living room, and Sloboština, and the whole country were shrouded in darkness, as black as the shadowy forest with its enormous evergreens that surrounded Twin Peaks. And not a single disco ball hanging from their branches.

At the very entrance, we were greeted by the familiar "Welcome to Twin Peaks" sign on the side of the road leading into this town where no one, not a single person, was innocent. We slowly approached the grieving Palmer family (who were anything but calm), Laura's high school friends, and the authorities in charge of the investigation. But, quickly upon entering the town, our Croatian couch hit up against the deck of this dark world, and a news crawl appeared under the subtitles, announcing air-raid sirens in Osijek, Daruvar, Pakrac, Karlovac, and Sisak, and warning that the list could soon include Zagreb—precisely when the horrifying details of Laura's murder were about to be revealed. My brother immediately rushed to the balcony and listened anxiously for nearby planes, while Special Agent Dale Cooper, after taking a sip of his "damn good coffee," continued to toil away in his investigation, not only into the mysterious circumstances and dark forces involved in Laura Palmer's homicide, but also into the firepower of the Yugoslav People's Army and Serb extremists, having no clue about this part of the script, which David Lynch and Mark Frost had never uttered a single word about to him. Parallel to new evidence, a fresh news crawl appeared with additions to the list of cities where aerial threats had already been announced. Cities were spawning, emerging in the lower right corner of the television screen and moving slowly toward the left, disappearing only to appear again. Meanwhile, the image of Laura's killer suddenly flashed before her mother's eyes, and it became critical to create a face sketch of the murderer, AIR-RAID SIREN IN SLAVONSKI BROD; Special Agent Cooper was then woken by an anonymous caller who assured him that he would reveal the killer at a confidential meeting with the agent at the hospital, RED-ALERT SIREN IN DUBROVNIK. As a police officer drew a portrait of the killer Mrs. Palmer described, Cooper raced to the hospital, where he was greeted by an eccentric one-armed man with a tattoo that read "fire walk with me" and was told that the killer was hiding in the basement, AIR-RAID SIREN IN NOVA GRADIŠKA. Cooper headed to the basement, where he discovered Bob the AIR-RAID SIREN IN VIROVITICA killer, and joining his fight against the forces of darkness was the town sheriff AIR-RAID SIREN IN VELIKA GORICA, which even we could make out from our balcony.

And, fortunately, after a series of skirmishes, the evil Bob, who had somehow taken on the appearance of Laura's father, was finally defeated, though his evil spirit remained, hovering over the residents of the town and anyone else who wound up there.

There was also an outrageously stupid twenty-five-year flash-forward of Cooper in a red room where Laura Palmer herself, wearing some sort of sexy-flexy outfit, supposedly whispered the killer's name in his ear—but that just left us confused. The important thing was that in the hospital basement of Twin Peaks, everything that needed to be resolved had indeed been resolved, and that Zagreb could, at the end of the day, calmly sink into its newly announced air-raid emergency, while its residents set out for the dark and damp layers beneath their hearths.

MAŠA KOLANOVIĆ

Dr. Kajfeš

"YOU SHOULD SCREW Bald Baby, then grab her wig in the middle of sex and put it on your head!"

When Svjetlana's Ken finished uttering these words to Dea's Barbie, the all-clear siren sounded and ended playtime, which was entering farce territory anyway. A Barbie farce.

Generally speaking, whenever we wore out the gameplay—after we'd changed our Barbies' clothes and combed their hair for the thousandth time, after all the intrigue had reached its denouement and, over coffee served on a small aluminum-can bar, our Barbies exchanged their final bits of gossip down to every last Barbie in the universe—it was then that Svjetlana's Ken (whom we called "Dr. Kajfeš," after the antisnoring aid in the commercials) would pull raunchy stunts like this latest episode, and we would launch into scolding Svjetlana while simultaneously dying of laughter. You never fully understood what Dr. Kajfeš was capable of, but he had an MO. More than anything, he loved to jump into the Barbies' beds uninvited, try on their clothes, whisper vulgar peasant jokes straight into their ears ("Hey girl, know why planes have flight attendants? So the planes can rise, *he he he*"), mount his head on a Barbie's body, or snore loudly, demonstrating the worthlessness of the anti-snoring aid he marketed as a traveling salesman (*hmph*, ultimately his snoring was just a pretext for Barbie to open the door, after which he would brutally rape her five times before she could say "cakes," and sometimes mistakenly "sex," which would make him even more unbridled). All this might not have been so heinous had Dr. Kajfeš not been the most abhorrent Ken you could ever come across in the entire *Illustrated History of Kens*, assuming there was such a thing, in times past or future. He wasn't of the Mattel race but made of an atrocious plastic that looked burnt, though he wasn't a Black Ken. And the cherry on top? One of his eyes was peeling off, and the fingers of his right hand were wrecked ever since Svjetlana's cousin Marijana had gnawed through them during one of her visits. That

MAŠA KOLANOVIĆ

fateful day left Svjetlana in a coma, because Marijana had ruined a sizable portion of her already-impoverished collection. It could have easily been the worst day in Svjetlana's life. Her tears came pouring like rain in a wet year, because aside from crippling her Ken, Marijana had stolen a little pair of (imitation) gold shoes *and* pressed a searing-hot iron against a pair of tiny synthetic leggings, and throughout the entire course of these deplorable events, Svjetlana's mother yelled at *Svjetlana*, and the poor girl had to keep playing with that idiot Marijana, who'd destroyed all the decent things she owned. If Svjetlana hadn't in that moment wished for a small coffin in her size, she would never wish for one. How could there not be a minimum age for playing with Barbies? If Legos were unsuitable for children "under 3 years old," why the *hell* couldn't Barbies be allotted the same? It should have been etched on their derrières in place of "Made in Taiwan"! Had a Mattel employee witnessed what nearly-three-year-old Marijana put Svjetlana's prized possessions through that day, they would have doubtlessly taken measures to protect the small, fragile creature from that neurotic elephant (in terms of relative size). Yes, it had truly been a horrific day, and yet some haters from our building, whom I will not name, were actually quite elated, because the situation allowed them to move up in the Top List of Barbies. The rest of us tried anything and everything to cheer up Svjetlana, like "Hey, your Ken"—ugh, out of desperation, we even called that deplorable thing *Ken*!—"could pretend he had an accident at work, and my Barbie could comfort him or something." But, no. Something had broken in our Svjetlana, and for a very long time no one could even begin to fathom what it was. Her

Ken—for the record, he was a fake Ken even before the terrible incident—had now become an irreparable catastrophe, and it was on her initiative that he transformed into "Dr. Kajfeš." With that, he became thoroughly disturbed and sexually wayward. But let me be frank: regardless of the extent to which this development interfered with our gameplay and made us want to strangle Svjetlana, our Barbies somehow, and only under certain circumstances, secretly reveled in this newly forged and oddly sexy identity that Dr. Kajfeš introduced to the game with all his shenanigans, sexual abuses, and overindulgences.

Such is the brief history of Dr. Kajfeš, who had barely pronounced his latest utterance when the all-clear siren blared and we stopped playing. Those sirens, after the seventh or eighth round, became something like a routine. When they sounded, we proceeded to the basement—although not everyone did so. Our parents were increasingly scarce down there, and eventually, they only joined us when the explosions grew

MAŠA KOLANOVIĆ

louder. As for us kids, before long we were liberated from our initial fears, and, little by little, we came to heed every siren, playing amidst explosions from distant Pokuplje and shots from the nearby Maršalka—the Marshal Tito Barracks. We went down to the basement even without the siren's command. There, despite the dust and the damp, everything seemed more special somehow. We had plenty of room to play, we each had a little key to our respective family storage units where we could stow our things, we decorated the walls, and we even had a plug for the boom box that the romantic evening hours required for playing slow songs. That war in Zagreb, when you grew used to it, wasn't actually all that bad. We gained our very own space for playing and we rarely attended school, which was more than favorable, especially to the underachievers.

And so, yet another round of sirens ended. We cleared away our Barbie apartments and headed back up to the real ones. Right then, Svjetlana approached and asked me for a favor. Apparently, Marijana would be visiting again that afternoon, posing an incalculable danger for her already-desecrated Barbie property. The feeling of terror brought on by Marijana's imminent arrival was equal to the terror induced by images of devastated houses whose still-standing walls were graffitied with "This is moine!" or "Croat-seized!" We had to think of something, of a way around these exceedingly precarious circumstances. Svjetlana already had a brilliant idea. She would come over, we would continue playing with our Barbies, and then she would "forget" the items she absolutely did not want falling into little Marijana's talons.

We arrived at my place. My whole family was home, and the news reports from the radio and the television were fizzing in every direction.

"Hi, Mom! Hi, Dad!"

The course and nature of the events demonstrate that this has nothing whatsoever to do with a political conflict oriented toward democracy, but rather a final attempt to destabilize and overthrow the legally and democratically elected Croatian government by now taking the form of an armed insurgency. The objective of this scenario was to introduce widespread confusion and an atmosphere of insecurity among the Croatian people, to incite disorder, terror, and, eventually, carry out a coup in order to establish a state of emergency in Croatia . . .

"Svjetlana's here—we're going to play in my room!"

MAŠA KOLANOVIĆ

... Under these circumstances, the Office of the President has considered the following: the outbreak of war in the Persian Gulf was intended to find the new Croatian government unprepared, and a final public statement by the Office of the President of the Republic of Croatia on the completion of the process of drawing up a confederal agreement that would allow a peaceful and democratic resolution for the constitutional and political crisis in Yugoslavia on the grounds of an agreement with the Office of the President of Yugoslavia ...

"We're hungry! What's there to eat?"

... Cardinal Franjo Kuharić addressed his fellow Croatian people: On the occasion of this difficult situation in Croatia, filled with unrest and intimidation, I would like to express to the Office of the President and the Government of the Republic of Croatia—on behalf of all Croatian bishops and myself—solidarity in the effort to preserve peace and freedom for all citizens ...

Needless to say, it was impossible to get anything resembling a response. But at least there was always Kinder Lada chocolate spread in the fridge, because:

a) it never spoiled
b) it filled up kids quickly
c) it was an excellent source of milk and calcium

We spread it over two slices of bread, following the example in the commercial: one with white chocolate, one with milk chocolate. This time, finally, in peace, because contrary to the present situation, my brother often hampered this undertaking by mixing the two sides before I even had a chance to dip my spoon. Two Kinder Lada slices and a glass of Dona blueberry juice fuller, we set about inventorying our Barbie property, which required:

a) checking whether everything was in its proper place
b) determining what needed to be protected from Marijana
c) reveling in the assortment of shimmery Barbie clothes at our fingertips

Svjetlana decided to "forget" all her Barbie shoes (a whole two pairs) at my place, some genuine Barbie clothes, and Dr. Kajfeš. I offered that "forgetting" Dr. Kajfeš could be interpreted as a highly suspicious act, since Marijana had previously shown a liking to him. But she simply couldn't take that great of a risk with Dr. Kajfeš, who was, after all, despite his revolting nature, her biggest

MAŠA KOLANOVIĆ

asset in the game—not to mention how deeply disappointed our Barbies would be, had Dr. Kajfeš endured something even more serious in a subsequent encounter with Marijana. Even so, it was important to note that the act would indeed incite a degree of suspicion. And just as our deliberations were coming to a close, and a resolution was within reach, my brother burst in and urged us *quick* to come to his room. In that room, our boom box was tuned to the news—the same news my mother and father were listening to in the living room, the same news blaring from nearly every apartment in the building. It appeared we were in the midst of an important moment, since our local radio station was transmitting through Radio Koper a statement from the leader of the Serb Democratic Party, Jovan Rašković.

. . . In a previous interview, I said that we would maybe even consider summoning the army for assistance. Maybe! And they made a big fuss about that and used the media to spread one big lie to the Croatian population in Croatia, the Croatian people—that I had supposedly summoned the army for assistance. I, under these circumstances, am neither summoning the army nor planning to summon the army, but if I do summon anyone for help, it'll be the Office of the President of Yugoslavia, because it's clear that one faction of the population of Croatia is being exposed to danger at present and that we must ask for help from the presidency of the Socialist Federal Republic of Yugoslavia. It is impossible for unarmed people—people armed with maybe a hunting rifle or assorted trophy weapons from historic battles, pistols mostly—it is impossible to summon tanks against those people, who are simply making a political plea; you can't summon the army against those people, or summon the special police, because that

would, as a matter of fact, be a declaration of war, and a declaration of war against one people in Yugoslavia is, in fact, a declaration of war against Yugoslavia. And, yeah, this is why we'll seek the intervention of the federal authorities. What that intervention will be, that's their thing. We'd actually like everything to go perfectly normal and in an orderly fashion to avoid any conflict. But we can't turn away Serbs who want to help us. We're not in favor of all kinds of assistance, but we are in favor of the kinds of assistance that help the rest of the Serb people. The Serb people are united. It has shown it. We, the Serb Democratic Party, have offered a platform for the unity of the Serb people and restored the unity of the Serb people, and the psychology of the Serb today, wherever he may be in Yugoslavia, recognizes that an attack on any Serb anywhere represents an attack on the entire Serb people.

It was not immediately clear what my brother wanted from us, but he explained everything before long—and, I have to admit, his idea was genius. His plan involved using his recording of Rašković's statement to put together a miniature news program

MAŠA KOLANOVIĆ

on our boom box, a short interview with the Serb Democratic Party in which we would weave questions around his responses. As soon as we came up with the script and assigned roles, we sprang into action. Svjetlana hummed the instrumental version of the theme song (*tanananananananana na-na-na* for "beautifulprecioussweet li-ber-ty!"), I presented the opening credits, and my brother posed the questions.

Dear listeners, this is HRT1, Croatian Radio Television's Premier Program. Today we spoke with the leader of the Serb Democratic Party, Jovan Rašković. The conversation was conducted over the phone, so please forgive us for the diminished quality of the recording. (This final note was meant to justify any subsequent incomprehensibility and the brief pauses occasioned by the assembly of each response.)

"Mr. Rašković, during your career as a party leader, have you ever considered killing the President of the Republic of Croatia, Dr. Franjo Tuđman?"

"With maybe a hunting rifle. And they made a big fuss about that."

"What is your reaction to the celebrations following the victory of the Croatian Democratic Union, HDZ—which included the roasting of oxen and the like?"

"That's their thing."

"Mr. Rašković, you are a psychologist. How do you treat Croatian patients?"

"Trophy weapons from historic battles, pistols mostly."

"Mr. Rašković, we have learned from a source that your beard is supposedly fake, and that it's made from Knin wool. Is that true?"

"One big lie."

"As a child, Mr. Rašković, what kind of toys did you like best?"

"Tanks."

"We heard, Mr. Rašković, that as a child, you—more accurately, you and your friend—fell into a pile of shit while playing in a garden. What did you do on that occasion?"

"Summoned the army for assistance."

"Mr. Rašković, where does all this hatred toward the President of the Republic, Dr. Franjo Tuđman, come from?"

"Because it's clear that one . . . is being exposed to danger."

"And does that, Mr. Rašković, imply being . . . sexually exposed?"

"Yeah."

"But how do you know this—Dr. Tuđman is a fine man, after all?"

"He . . . has shown it."

"Hmm, what is this 'it' that he has shown?"

"*Thing.*"

"You mean, *his* thing?"

"*Yeah.*"

"Mr. Rašković, how did the Office of the President of Yugoslavia react to that incident?"

"*An attack on any Serb anywhere represents an attack on the entire Serb people.*"

"And what is the final outcome of this unpleasant incident with Dr. Tuđman?"

"*A declaration of war.*"

"Thank you for joining us, Mr. Rašković, and goodbye. We sincerely hope you will join us again in the studio of Croatian Radio Television."

We were thrilled with our actualized project and played the recording repeatedly. As we rewound the tape to replay it once more, we realized our father was approaching the room, which visibly worried my brother. Basically, the tape he'd used to record our little interview with Jovan also contained a recording of our mother's confessions to a friend, and in said confessions, the primary receiver of criticism was our father. It was a remnant of my brother's previous media project, "The Candid Cassette," which entailed recording family conversations we were barred from attending. My brother would have

been royally screwed had our father learned of that project, and I doubt our mother would have spared him either, just as our parents were unlikely, given the disclosures on the tape, to spare each other. And then you'd have front-row tickets to chaos and despair! So my brother quickly grabbed a different cassette to camouflage our exploits under the guise of useful labor. It was an audiobook of Dobriša Cesarić and Dragutin Tadijanović reciting their own poems. As our father's hand turned the doorknob, and Dr. Kajfeš's fate lay unresolved on the rug, from my brother's room came the sounds of two tired, half-dead voices:

Čuj moje kucanje! Moj glas iz ... groba! ... Rastušje.
Hear my knock! My voice from ... the grave! ... Rastušje.

Dream Wedding

ALTHOUGH TEN DAYS had passed with no alerts, and even school had resumed, this particular day I had a premonition that a siren could blare at any moment. But a real siren—not the kind we learned to replicate with visible success, scaring passersby in the parking lot in front of our building. In truth, I don't know whether it was an actual premonition or a hope that it would go off so I could skip solfeggio and piano, which I hadn't practiced at all on the pretext of the sirens. The premonition took hold of me while I was watching television and waiting for my mother to come home from work and drive me to music lessons. In those days, all the channels were in a coma. Just News, News, News, and News, as part of a program called *Za slobodu* (For Freedom). But the German RTL channel never disappointed with its commercials, featuring a real purple Milka cow, a closer look at the production process of Mars and Snickers bars, a scaffold brimming with workers chiseling away at an enormous set of teeth until an equally enormous toothbrush armed with Colgate made them all redundant . . . That was in the daytime. Come night, German ladies with names like "Ruf Ann" would show their gargantuan boobs and direct viewers to a phone number that typically began with 666. But that late at night, we were forbidden even in the presence of our parents from turning on the television, especially when it had entered that period of turning itself on. So I casually made the rounds from *Za slobodu* to a few commercials on RTL, to a taste of Sky, and just when they aired Marko Perković Thompson performing "Čavoglave," my mother arrived and quickly fried up some eggs and French fries (my favorite), and we were off to music lessons before you could say *oh no*.

Attuned to my premonition, I decided to first deposit my Barbies in the basement—just in case, no harm done. And in the basement, everyone was of course preparing for the next development in the game—"everyone" being the lucky ones whose moms and dads never hounded them to take music lessons, or folk dancing, or English, or gymnastics, the lucky ones who (with the exception of school) could spend their time however and wherever they so desired, while my parents enrolled me in everything they possibly could, be it music, Latin and Greek... Whenever I objected, they arraigned me for being a vagrant who would rather do nothing but iron the ground beneath herself.

To make matters worse, that very day in the basement, Ana M.'s Ken and Dea's Barbie were supposed to marry. The wedding would be held in a small chapel erected from the remains of an old television that a neighbor had left in the basement in approximately the seventh century, from the looks of it, and there it had stood ever since, leaning against Ms. Munjeković's lidded plastic barrel of pickled cabbage. While I had been upstairs filling my music bag with sheet music—etudes, sonatas, and Marković's 555 *Selected Themes for Solfeggio*—the basement was already bustling with preparations for the Barbie wedding, which would be attended by several guests in the flesh and more than three hundred imaginary ones. Everything was set: there were the cars (shoes decorated with assorted ribbons), the confetti (rice), the limo for the newlyweds (an enormous white shoe that belonged to Ana M.'s father), the priest (Sanjica's Ken), the bouquet (clovers freshly picked in the little park area behind our building, which Dea's Barbie would throw for one lucky Barbie to catch), the bridesmaids, and an abundance of relatives and friends (who mostly just wanted to get plastered and gorge themselves at this most epic of Barbie celebrations to date).

To make matters more tense, Ken's best man was to be none other than Dr. Kajfeš, who, mere moments before the wedding, had tried every approach imaginable to talk Dea's Barbie out of marrying Ana's Ken, in the name of rescuing her from the jaws

MAŠA KOLANOVIĆ

of the humdrum life awaiting her with that cretin. But, no! That gold digger wouldn't hear a word of it. The precious turquoise pearls that Ana's Ken had bestowed upon her were more important than all the sincere love and wildflowers Dr. Kajfeš afforded her, bellowing Bijelo Dugme's hit, "Đurđevdan" (Saint George's Day) in his desperate and now hoarse voice under her window night after night, with an occasional performance of "Il' me ženi il' tamburu kupi, ja u nešto udarati moram" (Be my wife or get me a tambura, I need something to pluck) when all else had gone to hell. In more sentimental moments, he even ventured to write his own lyrics, which in painful solitude he set to music on his small plastic guitar. But she disparaged all those earnest feelings and made a calculated decision to marry for material gain.

Dr. Kajfeš had certainly had better days, but he feigned merriment with a forced smile that never left his face, just as it never left the faces of any of the Barbies, however serious—even deadly—the occasion. There were even attempted physical confrontations between Dr. Kajfeš and Ana's Ken, but they generally ended with Kajfeš losing another limb from his already rickety body. In the most recent altercation, his chewed-up right hand was so irreversibly wrecked that its every movement heightened the risk of falling out altogether. Following every incident, my Barbie comforted him with fake kisses, stamped into the air a centimeter from Kajfeš's burnt cheeks (similar to those I threw in the direction of my dead grandpa Viko at the behest of my aunt Marija, who made me obey the custom of kissing the dead at funerals). No wonder Dea's Barbie was disgusted by Kajfeš. After all, could you imagine the life she would lead with a man like that? She would inhabit a dismal valley of tears and suffering, subsisting on an assortment of disability and welfare benefits, whereas with Ana's Ken she could attain the life she had always coveted: heaps of plastic pearls and small items Made in Taiwan, China, Malaysia, or the Philippines, possessions that were an undeniable necessity for a modern woman like Barbie. Plus, after the wedding, Ana's Ken had promised Dea's Barbie they would spend their honeymoon in the Bahamas. (The Bahamas being a turquoise washbasin paired with a beach umbrella made out of the domed lid of a fruity ice cream cup from the Ledo store.)

There, Dea's Barbie would change in and out of a thousand flashy outfits for every segment of the day, idly sip cocktails poolside at the hotel, and enjoy cheap massages from the locals, playing the part of Poolside Vacation Barbie till death do them part. Dr. Kajfeš and Ana's Ken settled their dispute, for the most part, after they got absolutely wasted and became the best of friends again—the very path that had led them to the best-man arrangement. And although he would eventually become entangled with many other Barbies, Dr. Kajfeš never truly got over Dea's Barbie.

This was the sequence of wedding-related events slated to play out on that particular day, while my Barbie and I, thanks to stupid music lessons, were unable to attend the nuptial festivities. The very image of a poor, miserable wretch, I set about groundlessly depositing my things in our storage space, while everyone else was deep in their celebratory element. Kajfeš had even procured a small Croatian flag attached to a toothpick that he intended to wave out of the car, and Dea suggested the idea of having an imaginary tamburitza orchestra, which was now on its way to pick up and escort the bride. There were even traditional wedding gifts (Lego bricks wrapped in colorful paper and tied with thin ribbon). Borna's Skipper was capturing all of this on her tiny video camera, which wasn't a genuine Barbie camera, but one that Borna, the lucky fellow, had chanced upon in his Kinder chocolate egg. I saw it all with my own eyes before glumly exiting the basement and heading toward our blue Renault 4, where my mother had already been anxiously honking the horn to get me to pick up the pace or else be late for solfeggio. While from the basement you could hear the sounds of the lively commotion of the guests and the hooting and hollering of the invisible Barbie tamburitza players, I entered the blue Renault 4, which drove me straight to Pavao Markovac Music School, Victims of Fascism Square #9. When I tried again in the car to speak up with respect to my own interests and ambitions, which ran counter to those of my parents, my mother began yelling that I was to shut it at once, because she could have written three doctoral dissertations in the time she spent in the car waiting for me to finish music lessons. The remainder

of the drive toward the city center passed in silence. I tried to imagine the activities currently underway in the basement. The bridal party was likely en route to the television, the car horns were blaring, the musicians performing, and the bride enraptured by her dream Barbie wedding, which would purportedly be the happiest day of her life, while Dr. Kajfeš sang and sang, waving his toothpick flag, whereas in reality his soul was stinging with the pain of watching his beloved marry another. Perhaps, in the heat of the moment, he would try to pierce Ana's Ken in the eye with his Croatian toothpick and thus transform this dream wedding into a bloodfest. But no

doubt a small security detail was assigned to keep Kajfeš in check. In my mind, I was underground, while aboveground there suddenly rang out that recognizable sound. It had gone off! The air-raid siren had gone off, just as I had predicted! I can't deny the fact that I was actually quite scared—it was the first time the siren had found me outside Sloboština—but on the inside of my outwardly unhappy self, I was still in one way or another relieved that music lessons were definitely out of the picture for today. Plus, my Barbie property was safe. My mother, in the meantime, completely transformed into a stuntwoman: with one hand she turned the wheel 360 degrees around the Art Pavilion, while with the other she pushed me under the backseat for fear of snipers. In those days, Zagreb was saturated with snipers. Ms. Munjeković said that Ms. Staneković told her that Ms. Pilko accidently dropped a plastic bag while she was exiting the tram and just as she was bending over to pick it up, a woman behind her was shot by a sniper. Our neighbor Mr. Horvat heard that Mamutica was full of Četniks and Fifth Columnists who held everything at gunpoint between lowered blinds, including those of us who played in front of our building when we grew bored of the basement. Mr. Horvat said that all those buildings— the Mamutica, the Super Andrija, the Raketa—were chock-full of Serbs and Četniks.

Crouched there under the backseat, I watched the fragmented moving images of the city during this drive that was beginning to make me nauseous. My mother was pressing through city traffic in the direction of Novi Zagreb. When we finally arrived in Sloboština, I rushed straight to the basement, and boy was there something to see. The wedding was already at an advanced stage. Half of the Barbies were drunkenly lying face down at their tables, and Dea's Barbie was unwrapping a heap of wedding gifts, while Dr. Kajfeš was climbing onto a table, hand in hand with Ana's Ken, singing Thompson's "Čavoglave":

Stići će vas naša ruka i u Srbiji...
Our hand will reach you in Serbia too...

Borna's Skipper

ZUJI, ZVEČI, ZVONI, zvuči—buzzing, banging, ringing, clanging,
Šumi, grmi, tutnji, huči—rustling, thundering, rumbling,
  howling,
To je jezik roda moga!—hear the language of my people!
Zuji, zveči, zvoni, zvuči, šumi, grmi, tutnji, huči, to je jezik
roda moga!

And again—buzzing, banging, ringing, clanging, rustling, thundering, rumbling, howling, hear the language of my people!

We only had one afternoon to commit this entire song to memory, but I was completely immobilized by *buzzing, banging, ringing, clanging, rustling, thundering, rumbling, howling*. I had no idea whether the fourth word was followed by wailing, or howling, or hailing, or some other natural phenomenon, and there were questions I still needed to write complete-sentence responses to in my notebook regarding this so-called pedigree poet of volcanic power, whose picture in my reader my brother had decorated with sunglasses and "Metallica" on his forehead. Besides, who could concentrate on homework when my brother in his room spent the entire afternoon listening to the radio? The enemy radio no less, for which I nearly snitched on him to our parents. Apart from some static, our small boom box impressively picked up Radio Glina, which, following the withdrawal of the Yugoslav People's Army from the barracks in Croatia, offered musical programming for the newly declared Srpska autonomna oblast (Serb Autonomous Region) of Krajina.

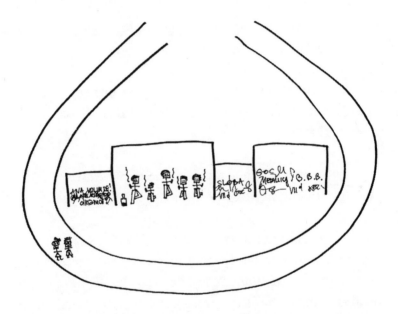

Svi ti prete Krajino ti uspravno stojiiiiš, celom svetu sada reci da ih se ne bojiiiš...
Četnik do četnika junak do junaka ne plaše se boja ni ljutih bitakaaa...

Bez otadžbine na Krfu živeh ja, ali sam ponosno klico živela Srbijaaa...

Nosila ti Drina sto Mudžahedina svaki dan, oj svaki dan oj...

Everyone threatens you, Krajino, but you stand taaaall,
Now go and tell the whole world you're not afraid at aaaaall...
No Četnik, no hero, would let some vicious battle
   intimidate...
Exiled in Corfu, I proudly cheered, "Serbia we must
   liberate!"...
May the river Drina carry a hundred Mujahideen every day,
   oy, every day, oy...

—interspersed with a constant "Krajin-o to Toky-o!" supplemented by the charming radio announcer. Exactly half an hour remained to memorize buzzing, banging, ringing, clanging, etc., because at exactly 18:00, Borna would come by so we could go to choir practice. Borna and I were the only ones from our building enrolled in choir, which was conducted by our music teacher, Mr. Kutnjak, with the accompaniment of a tamburitza orchestra. We were rehearsing for the Day of Education recital, although its status was on-again, off-again, depending on the alerts. Plus, if you attended choir practice, you earned extra credit with Kutnjak, which equated to a higher overall grade in music. And choir was totally fine, because unlike in music class, not only was there no instrument to practice at home, but it also afforded us the opportunity to circle after rehearsal to the back of the school, where at night all the best-looking eighth graders (*yes!*) hung out, among whom you could, like sprats among sharks, spot a few fourth graders.

That day I might have, given all my Croatian language homework, actually had a valid excuse to skip rehearsal, but I went anyway because we were supposed to try on the new embroidered vests for the performance. As I was wrestling thus with buzzing, banging, and so on and so forth, Borna rang on the intercom and I was

MAŠA KOLANOVIĆ

saved by the bell. My brother always snickered when Borna rang for me on the intercom or asked to speak to me on the phone. But to all the girls in our building, Borna was a great friend and the only boy in Sloboština we knew of who played with Barbies. It was mainly the other boys in the neighborhood who didn't much care for Borna, and mostly because of his high-pitched voice, and because he played with Barbies. One time, when we were playing on the raised sewage vent out front, a boy from #15, led by Salih, ran toward our building with the intention of beating up Borna.

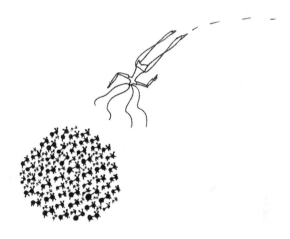

But us girls saved him by quickly hiding him in the garbage can storage shed and locking it, and Borna consequently dodged mortal danger. Salih spent the next while furiously kicking the shed while Borna hid behind the container. Then Salih, in a fit of rage, disturbed a pair of anthills we had tended like a small zoo in front of the building, and ravaged a pair of Barbie homes on the sewage vent—all of which could have led to damage of untold proportions had Mr. Horvat not appeared and chased them off.

Aside from a few razed apartments that we were able to restore fairly quickly, the damage was modest. Only Ana P.'s Barbie ended up headfirst in the disturbed anthill, which was tantamount to a tragedy of ant proportions. Playing on the sewage vent became truly hazardous in the light of this incident, so our discovery of the basement during the war proved to be a

much safer option for Borna and the Barbies. But back when I said Borna was the only boy we knew who played with Barbies, I should have immediately mentioned that Borna never actually had a Barbie of his own. He was, namely, known for his genuine Bathtime Fun Skipper, who boasted an endless range of toiletries for showering, perfuming, shampooing, blow-drying, and brushing, in addition to a terry-cloth bathrobe with an embroidered "S" and a towel she often wore tied in a turban after pretend-washing her hair. (In hindsight, everything in Barbie World was "pretend," but some things were more real than others.) That Skipperette was really something, and she seemed all but made for Borna. No one could even imagine Borna owning a Barbie or a Ken, because the Skipper somehow perfectly complemented his stature and voice (aside from his high-pitched voice, Borna wore thick glasses and suffered from acne). Then one day his aunt in Italy sent him some sort of Vespa for his Skipper. The Vespa wasn't genuine Mattel, but it was perfect nonetheless. A small battery-powered red one with remote control.

During a subsequent argument between Borna and his brother, Krešo (who lived with Borna's father, since their parents were divorced), we found out the Vespa hadn't been made for the Skipper at all; it originally belonged to some Italian policeman whom Borna had unseated and replaced with his Skipper. No one knew where that Italian policeman ended up, but it was alleged that he had an unbelievably small head and remained fixed in a sitting position; hence, none of our Barbies mourned this dwarfish eyesore. The main thing was: this Italian trash had his Vespa impounded, and that Vespa perfectly suited Borna's Skipper. The experience of taking it for a spin with Borna's Skipper was truly incredible. Although she sometimes lost control of the vehicle and the joyride ended in a minor accident somewhere over by the rat poison at the far end of the basement (where news programming for Croatian television was routinely presented by Dr. Kajfeš), Borna's Skipper was, on the whole, an excellent driver, bypassing obstacles down to the smallest bit of wood, spit, or mouse droppings like a bona fide stuntwoman. But behind this stuntwoman facade, Borna's Skipper had a secret—namely, her unrequited love for Dr. Kajfeš. It was revealed when Borna and Svjetlana were playing by themselves at Svjetlana's, but since Svjetlana related everything to Dea, in the hope of making Kajfeš seem like a bigger deal in the eyes of Dea's Barbie than he in fact was, the rest of us found out about it quickly thereafter, only we hid our knowing from Borna.

The underage Skipper and Dr. Kajfeš were in the middle of a scene set during a school skiing trip that unfolded on the snowy heights of Jahorina. Kajfeš was the physical education teacher and the supervisor of the entire grade, whose top student was Borna's Skipper. And as the small class set out toward this imaginary Jahorina's snowy peaks (coated in crumbled Styrofoam), Borna's Skipper and Mr. Kajfeš (who simultaneously played the part of Bendable-Leg Ken in this skiing scene) were already getting acquainted at the restaurant on the small train. Mr. Kajfeš *this*, Mr. Kajfeš *that* . . . she was brownnosing him for merely a few more points of extra credit (three would result in an A).

MAŠA KOLANOVIĆ

Everyone was quite familiar with Kajfeš's inability to redirect his eyes (eye, rather, considering one of them had faded) away from the little blonde nymphs, but as the grade-level supervisor, he had to be very discreet and avoid getting caught stealing furtive glances at their little breasts, which swung left and right during dodgeball, volleyball, and track. He was simply unattracted to the middle-aged hags in the teachers' lounge, all

those graying instructors of Croatian language, history, and mathematics often played by dusty old Barbies with unfortunate haircuts. Who can blame him, when before him frolicked all those little nuggets of juicy chicken meat? At the time, Kajfeš purportedly even had a family, which in fact merely served to mask his taste for Skippers. With consideration to Kajfeš *and* the Skippers, the attraction was certainly reciprocated. He was, after all, the physical education teacher and the grade-level supervisor, regardless of the actual quality of his pedagogy; he could climb ropes and vault over the pommel horse, in addition to making assessments (albeit in his particular style). Besides, the Skippers had evidently little to choose from in a class full of half-mutated boys with acne; hence, circumstance had forced them to look to Kajfeš as though he were their own personal idol, who was, at the end of the day, a semifledged man. These were the conditions under which Borna's Skipper came to covertly harbor strong feelings for Mr. Kajfeš, the physical education teacher and grade-level supervisor. This sometimes happened to geeks like Borna's Skipper. And let me set things straight here and now: these were not feelings Borna and Svjetlana had for each other; these were feelings shared exclusively between Borna's Skipper and Dr. Kajfeš (rather, the physical education teacher and grade-level supervisor).

Venturing outside the little Balkan Barbie Express train, Kajfeš and Borna's Skipper also spent extensive time on the Styrofoam ski slopes (where they chased each other through the snow in the style of the music video for "Last Christmas I Gave You My Heart") and in the hotel restaurant (which, considering the class budget, was unsurprisingly unimpressive compared to the luxurious Barbie hotels in the catalog), until the third day of the school trip, when Kajfeš proposed that they break away from the rest of the class and spend a couple of days at a more expensive hotel that offered a sauna and massage services—Kajfeš's treat! He knew this cheap trick would win her over, because Borna's Skipper jumped at every opportunity to show off her Bathtime Fun gear. So, they made arrangements: reconvene in the hotel lobby, 20:15 sharp. As a more serious man and grade-level supervisor, Kajfeš had to watch the evening news and check the weather and war conditions for the following day. Skipper, in the meantime, made herself up, applied some (imitation) expensive perfume, and headed down to the lobby a smidge earlier. Once Kajfeš arrived, the two set off for the sauna and massage. But what actually transpired there remained an enigma that even Dea couldn't resolve, no matter how hard she tried. It was alleged that Svjetlana's mother came home from work and Svjetlana had to go do her homework, but, for all intents and purposes, Borna's Skipper became infatuated with Kajfeš, and sometime later he supposedly realized that none of it made much sense—the whole affair could be exposed, the press could pick it up, and then there goes physical education, let alone his position as grade-level supervisor, which did grant him a wage bump, however small. In that time, Borna's Skipper only fell deeper and deeper into the grip of longing for her teacher and secretly hoped the day would come, after graduating high school, when Kajfeš would leave his wife (if she even existed) and Skipper would sink into his embrace and live there happily ever after. But before graduation, there was lo-ho-hoads of Barbie time expressed in human hours ...

All in all, this was how things stood with Borna's Skipper. Borna played with us often, plus he and I were enrolled together in that choir with Kutnjak, which brought us even closer in a way. At Borna's birthday party, I was first to arrive and last to go (Borna and I were up late choreographing Magazin's "Sve bi seke ljubile mornare"—the only ballad that truly communicated a girl's yearning to kiss a sailor). And at rehearsal that very same day, we received our red embroidered vests to be worn over a white collared shirt for the recital; then afterward, Borna and I went on a walk around the school, which, given the state of the nation, was brisk and short. It was solely for my benefit that Borna, a true friend, circled round the school, because I wanted to catch a glimpse of Ivica Glavinić, my crush. (For his birthday, I gifted Ivica a bullet, which I stole from my brother's collection of military paraphernalia, wrapped in a small heart.)

MAŠA KOLANOVIĆ

The evening passed calmly, and I needed to return home a bit earlier to run through all the buzzing, banging, ringing, clanging once more ... But when I arrived home, something terrible happened. My mother received a telephone call from none other than an office in the Yugoslav People's Army, announcing that her son had trespassed on the property of the Marshal Tito Barracks in Travno, but she had no reason to worry—he was safe and sound and she could pick him after the Croatian police finished his paperwork.

My mother and father were in shock. "I thought they'd left and I just wanted to collect some bulle—!" were the only words my brother managed to pronounce before he was slapped (by Mom) when our parents took him back into their custody.

Our home echoed, for a long time indeed, with the buzzing, banging, groaning, yelling, ringing, thundering, crushing language of my people.

The Feather Collectors

ON THOSE GLOOMY and overcast days during a kind of ceasefire, when the Yugoslav People's Army began withdrawing from all the barracks in the Republic of Croatia, we industriously collected feathers. Like scattered beads of a costume necklace, we spread across Sloboština's meadows and the surrounding turf, with the clearly defined targets shared by most feather collectors.

We mostly stumbled upon ordinary gray pigeon feathers, which were everywhere. We collected them from the concrete sidewalks plastered with chewing gum; from the little park behind our building, heavily mined with excrement of the canine variety; from a low wall littered with cigarette butts behind the halfwit house (the Rehabilitation Center, Novi Zagreb branch); from

the small field behind the school, strewn with all manner of trash, along with the odd syringe. Equally common were those enormous pitch-black feathers from the crows that lined the telephone lines dotting the empty space between Sloboština and Velikogorička Road. Beside the occasional colorful parakeet feather I wangled in an altogether violent fashion, frightening the bird into a frantic flight from one end of the cage to the other, the biggest feathery prize of all included the speckled hen and the white goose. We gathered those by sneaking into the yard of a house with a chicken coop, located a little farther from our building. In such moments, the industrious little beads transformed into little commandos invading a Serb home.

Even though in the moment of trespassing I felt uneasy and scared (what if the man and woman came out of the house and set loose the fierce dog the sign at the entrance warned about?), those unlawful entries fell into the category of thrilling, stomach-tingling events. They were meticulously planned and carried out during the homeowners' afternoon break, which they spent lying on a bed behind a window with floral curtains, in a slumber so deep it rivaled the sleep of the dead.

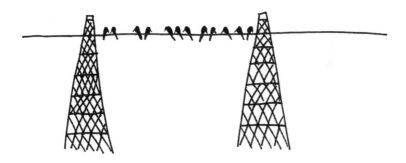

Everyone participated in those invasions—everyone but Sanjica, who remained traumatized by chicken coops ever since her cousin Tanja from Zagorje recruited her to help slaughter a chicken. Sanjica had, in that event, been forced to participate in the brutal act, which ended in an utter chaos of feathers, with the girls only just managing to hack halfway through one orange leg using a large serrated bread knife before the aunt rushed over to finish the job. But our own dirty work was different. The poultry in the latter case remained utterly untouched and the feather collecting was executed without so much as a single drop of blood. We simply needed to gather as many of the fallen feathers as we could and deliver them to the little old lady on the tenth floor in building #13.

In exchange, she generously rewarded us with coins, reserving paper money for when a colorful feather or two surfaced from among the heap of gray and black. Aside from my contribution, colorful feathers additionally arrived from Tea, who deplumed her budgie using a method similar to mine. The old lady bought the feathers from us as raw material for her art. She

was sculpting an enormous feathered bird in honor of Dr. Franjo Tuđman, and our participation in her project seemed like an exceedingly favorable opportunity to bolster our rather meager allowances in those somber and stingy days. Our parents, however, highly disapproved of any contact with the strange old lady, and, after they warned us about the balefulness of this exchange of goods in the interests of our humble but steady and stable budgets (from the perspective of the parents), the campaign to maintain this additional source of income became strictly confidential. Which wasn't exactly easy, considering we had to deal with highly active independent contractors. Although we could have never foreseen such an arrangement, we were joined in the feather-collecting business by our archenemies, Salih and Alija—whose name wasn't actually Alija, but we called him, along with his brothers *and* his sisters, "Alija" (after the Bosnian Muslim president) because they'd all moved from Bosnia. Alija was an expert handler of poultry, which remained calm when he entered the yard (unlike when we made an appearance) and merely pecked toward the Kviki gric salted crackers he deftly sprinkled. Concurrently, the group from our building, in partnership with Salih, raced to collect as many feathers from that muddy yard full of filth and old junk as quickly as we could. While we collected the feathers, Alija simultaneously deterred a savage gaggle of geese from rushing at us. But this entire deal with the feathers had to remain inconspicuous, given the multiple warnings we'd received. Our smuggling operation was successfully camouflaged by our playing with Barbies on the raised sewage vent in the front of the building, so our parents could keep us in their

crosshairs and therefore suspect nothing. During playtime, we would attend to our temp work in shifts with Salih and Alija, then cash in the feathery spoils at the home of the old lady, whose tiny blue eyes gleamed with pleasure deep in the wrinkly hollows of her bony face.

And while a troop of special envoys was engaged in a covert mission, on the larger of the sewage vents Dr. Kajfeš fell into his usual ecstasies, albeit this time amplified further by the fact that no one took this quasi playtime seriously anymore, since it now primarily served to screen far more important developments. Namely, Dr. Kajfeš was suddenly stricken with multiple personality disorder, and to make matters worse, none of those spawned could offer him any professional help, considering he was the only licensed doctor.

One moment he was Bruce Lee, defending Barbie with his karate moves against invisible rapists (a long list on which he himself appeared); a moment later he was Rudolph Valentino in oriental dress, tying up Barbie with barbed wire and tickling the soles of her feet with his freshly collected feathers; a moment after that he was Robin Hood, plundering the homes of envoys who were away, and then abruptly he would begin smashing all the stolen goods like Jimi Hendrix and his electric guitar; until the following moment when he transformed into Vojislav Šešelj and invaded Barbie's bed, cooing in her ear, "Oh, Bavbie, my heavt, my Gveatev Sevbia." Everything under the sun and more was on full display after Dr. Kajfeš's diagnosis. He was Batman, and Spider-Man, and Postman Duje "who loves and 'spects you" ("što voli vas i štuje"), and Aca je uvek Aca ("Aca will be Aca"), and Danko Bananko ("Bananaman"), and Tuđman, and Branko rat-tat-tat Kockica (who frequented Barbie parties and spied on the counterrevolutionary activities of party officials before he was himself caught in a trap). And all this in the span of half a minute! The second half of this selfsame minute would begin with his transformation into Slobodan Milošević, whereby he proposed a rational state, which immediately gave rise to a massive gathering of protesters shouting "Slobo, Saddam!" with a masked Kajfeš at the helm. Slobo would then mutate into Superman Serb Kajfeš and, wearing Skipper's skintight aerobics leotard with Barbie's favorite tablecloth draped on his back, bomb demonstrators with explosives made from pebbles that had gotten stuck in the slats of the sewage vent.

During this period of Kajfeš's personal hell, which exuded the darkest sides of his personality in the guise of famous, and infamous, stars and heroes, a group of special envoys set about delivering a fresh batch of feathers. This time I joined the delegation riding the elevator to the tenth floor, where, in anticipation of our arrival, the door to the little apartment stood ajar.

The apartment secreted a rather unpleasant smell with no resemblance to the counterfeit perfumes off Konjščinska Street, which were an absolute hit. The wrinkled old woman was expecting us, engrossed in a scale model of a large bird skeleton covered in glued feathers. This strange lady's apartment was brimming with not only a vast array of embroidered scenes on its walls, but also an assortment of stuffed birds placed around an armchair reupholstered in dark-green velvet. She told us these were hunting trophies that belonged to her husband, who had once upon a time been a well-known hunter, but then under communism he ended up in one of the numerous pits with unidentified victims later unearthed as skeletons. Whenever she spoke of her late husband, a melancholy air enveloped the old woman and her blue beady eyes brimmed with tears. Nowhere in the entire neighborhood or surrounding area was there a soul lonelier than our little granny,

MAŠA KOLANOVIĆ

albeit others called her a crazy witch who should be avoided. Us kids were her only friends, even if our favorite part of this friendship was the pocket change she granted us, although on this particular occasion we also spotted two paper bills among the coins for the handful of colorful feathers delivered that day, which prompted us all to grow feathers of our own and fly to the corner shop to buy supplies for a proper feast: seven blueberry-flavored Gringos, ten Bazookas, five small Kinder Ladas, and five Yupi juice boxes—all of which we intended to devour after we rushed back to our spot on the sewage vent. Yippee!

In the meantime, the second shift of feather collectors had finished delivering a fresh shipment, so everyone gathered together for this picnic break on the sewage vent. Everyone, that is, but Kajfeš, whose personal drama had newly enlisted Ana M.'s Ken and thereby converted his personal drama to a two-person drama of unprecedented scale. Those two were now jointly suffering from serious mental illnesses with no known cause or cure, which meant that one moment they were Milli Vanilli lip-synching with choreographed dance moves; the next moment they were *Miami Vice*, with Kajfeš playing the Black cop; then they were Pat and

Mat from *A je to!* (Pat & Mat!), ruining already vandalized and ransacked apartments; then Mladić and Karadžić, massacring plastic civilians; then Lolek and Bolek, athletes at the Olympics in the Czech Republic...

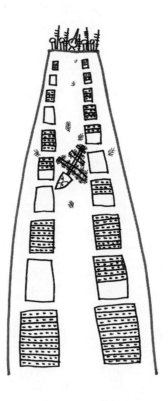

Since there was no way to put an end to this doubled madness unfolding at the large sewage vent, a new delegation of special envoys was assembled for the purposes of holding disciplinary hearings to address Svjetlana and Ana M.—an arrangement that required my participation as an impartial observer in immaculate white, thanks to Ariel laundry detergent. Following this order, Kajfeš and Ana M.'s Ken plummeted onto the sewage vent and fell silent. After the fall, all three of us—Svjetlana, Ana M., and I—headed for the chicken coop, even though the sky was getting darker and darker and it was only a matter of time before the storm would scramble Operation Feathers. Surrounded by gray, like geese in fog, we set out in the direction of the small farmstead, traversing only a short distance before we caught sight of Salih and Alija, who, under pressure from a gaggle of geese, were running toward us. Backdropped by bellowing thunderclouds, chased by the frantic white flock, we bolted together like an eccentric bunch of marathon runners back in the direction of the building, where an enormous feathered bird skeleton dove off the tenth floor.

Trip to Travno

WHILE KAJFEŠ WAS in the midst of belting out "24 mila baci" (24,000 Kisses), with guitar accompaniment, below my Barbie's balcony, Svjetlana had a bathroom emergency. This was otherwise a scene from our Roman Holiday Barbie game, which we modeled after the eponymous image in the catalog. For the scenography, we only needed one postcard from Rome and scores of little outfits for Barbie to change into every second of her romantic trip in the Italian capital. In front of the picture of the Roman Colosseum—the back of which read, "It's very beautiful in Rome. Love, Mom and Dad"—my Barbie and Dr. Kajfeš spent hours strolling hand in hand, enjoying pizzas and lasagnas, and riding around town on an imaginary Vespa during the daylight hours and, come nighttime, in a carriage pulled by two well-brushed Barbie stallions with purple hairpins in their pink braids.

It was our favorite scenario in the game Svjetlana and I played without the other girls and Borna. While we played in my room, my brother and his friends were in his room, which reeked of sneakers and sweat. And in the second I rushed over to Svjetlana to toss a roll of toilet paper through the opening above the bathroom door in that, as ever, ill-timed exhaustion of supplies, Roman Holiday Barbie, following an intervention staged by my brother and his friends, transformed into Nudist Camp Barbie in the very heart of Rome!

To avoid any further conflict, we relocated to the basement to continue our Italian honeymoon. But in the basement we found Ana P.'s brother drilling his buddies in the course of a paramilitary exercise. The boys were running around and, in their mutating pubescent voices, repeating loudly after Ana's brother:

"We'll overthrow the JNA!"

"We'll overthrow the JNA!"

"Down with SAO Krajina!"

"Down with SAO Krajina!"

We'd seen enough. We hurried out of the basement to the little park behind our building, to prevent the nudist camp from transforming into a military camp fenced in with barbed wire. Behind the building, my Barbie and Kajfeš could finally dance in peace to one of countless slow numbers by Eros Ramazzotti.

But even this moment was short-lived, as it was quickly interrupted by Svjetlana's mother, who appeared on their balcony and ordered Svjetlana to go fetch her father from the bocce court in Travno and tell him to come home at once—an order she extended to Svjetlana because it wasn't exactly safe to wander about with a war underway, even though Travno had, after the Yugoslav National Army finally pulled its troops out of the Maršalka barracks, become much safer.

Naturally, as a loyal friend, I accompanied her on this journey, which we embarked on with our Barbie belongings in tow. We left Sloboština slowly but surely, and once we passed the little park, then the parking lot, and the sledding hills, we found ourselves at the enormous intersection separating Sloboština

from Travno and Dugave. Cars raced by, but we were thrilled; in those days there was no straying anywhere outside Sloboština or its surrounding fields, let alone traversing that monstrous intersection by ourselves. In days past we would board the Sloboština bus on the penultimate stop and disembark at the final stop, or, with adult accompaniment, visit a local library on the neighboring block, but that was as far as we ever ventured.

This independent departure to Travno, and, moreover, in such uncertain times, thus seemed like a proper excursion—although, admittedly, not as momentous as a trip to Pioneer City, which had in the meantime been indefinitely suspended. Like two hobbits we crossed the vast intersection and glanced back at Sloboština; its buildings, laid out as they were in a circle, now conjured up Dubrovnik's old city walls, and the two buildings of Mamutica that we were on a collision course with resembled mammoth cruise ships. Shortly after we stepped onto the territory of Travno, on the green space at the foot of Mamutica, near the gardens and smaller fields, was the bocce court where Svjetlana's father played bocce with his friends, who spoke an array of dialects.

As we approached, Svjetlana's father scrambled to place his beer on an old oven—which complemented a few old refrigerators and washing machines and served well as furniture—then cheerfully walked over to greet us. When Svjetlana relayed her mother's message, he handed us money for ice cream and told us to take a little stroll and inform her mother that we hadn't seen him on the bocce court with a beer in his hand. Elated that we had ice cream money, we set out toward Mamutica and swiftly arrived at the plateau that connected the two buildings with a corner store, a library, the Travno Community Center

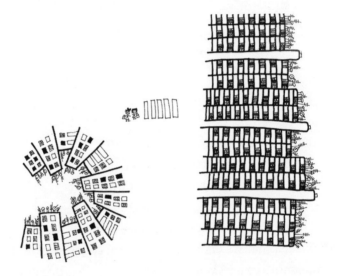

(whose windows were sandbagged), a newsstand, a Zeko knitwear shop, and two gargantuan concrete nostrils that served as entrances to the underground parking lot. At the corner store, we bought ourselves two Snow White ice cream bars and commenced our tour of the plateau, where we observed other kids playing hopscotch, dodgeball, and the gumi-gumi jump-rope game. But what grabbed our attention was a colorful heap on a hillock behind the plateau. We tossed our Snow Whites (which we'd licked clean) and headed for the hillock, where three girls were playing with Barbies. The finger of fate and adventure guided us to wash up with our Barbie belongings on that island hill (although I should clarify that the only bona fide island Barbie could wash up on was Manhattan). There, we beheld a sight as yet unseen—one of the girls was holding an honest-to-goodness Black Barbie!

Prior to this, we'd only ever seen Black Barbie in the catalog, where she was presented either as a version of White Barbie—one appearing in a small image, the latter in a large one—or as her good friend (because not everyone could be like Barbie, but they could at least be her good friend). While the other two girls who had White Barbies in their hands faintly scowled at our arrival, the Black Barbie welcomed us warmly to that green isle in Mamutica's vicinity. How lucky we had our gear with us and could jump right into the game. We were enchanted by all the little things that hadn't been routine in our Barbie sphere—especially the Black Barbie, whom we'd never had a chance to see in the flesh, let alone to hold her. The Black Barbie was the same as the White one, except Black. She was a United Colors of Benetton Shopping Teresa, sent by the girl's relatives in Australia because she already had eight White Barbies. Teresa had all the genuine little Benetton outfits, and their vivid colors impeccably complemented her dark complexion. The other two girls had a Superstar Festival Barbie and a Fashion Play Barbie with a multitude of genuine *easy to dress* and *easy to undress* clothes. All three were eager to see what we had in store, but to avoid immediately frightening them off with Kajfeš, we first showed them my Crystal Barbie, who impressed everyone with her glittery, festive dress. Then from inside the bag and into the light of day came Dr. Kajfeš. A thousand shiny tuxedos couldn't correct the first impression he gave. It was obvious straightaway that what they were witnessing was a rather ugly fake Ken, but, with no other prospects, the girls from Travno could only accept him as he was. And not long after he joined the game, Kajfeš revealed his other redeeming qualities.

He behaved unusually gentlemanly toward all the Barbies, with particular regard for Black Teresa. Oh, he was a charmer, all right. A charmer and a tramp. He and Teresa would spend hours surfing on polished Ledo ice cream sticks, braving the king

MAŠA KOLANOVIĆ

waves incoming from Mamutica. Most of their time they spent in a small cocktail bar under straw palms. Kajfeš would rub her already-tanned shoulders with special uv lotions and massage her feet, which throbbed with pain from all the high heels and appeared anatomically as though they were stuck on their tiptoes. Then, out of sheer fondness, he would bury her in the sand (the soil on the hill) and dig her back out again in time for a sandy sunset stroll, two dark silhouettes on a pink-and-orange backdrop, leaving a trail in the shallows where heart-shaped waves swept across their feet. Concurrent with these developments, my Barbie mingled with the two others and flew through outfit changes without stop, delighting in all the new combinations of clothing and other Travnotrinkets. Things between Teresa and Kajfeš were clearly moving in an all-too-familiar direction, even though less than an hour before, in Rome, Kajfeš had pledged those same mountains and valleys to my Barbie, singing into her ear "insieme unite unite Europe" and other canzones. But then, during one of the sandy pink sunset strolls under imaginary palms, Kajfeš went a step further: he proposed to Teresa and confessed he had come all the way from the Pacific to Travno on his surfboard without ever once seeing a beauty like her. And although the wedding had to transpire quite spontaneously at the Pineapple Hotel located on the small turquoise isle, fate was tragically altered by an air-raid siren, which cued us to quickly pack our things and excuse ourselves without saying goodbye. The girls from the hillock darted for cover toward their building, while Svjetlana and I scurried toward Slobošti-na's walls, into our own catacombs. When everything passed, we recounted our Travno adventure for days.

In that interval, Black Teresa gazed longingly at the open sea in the direction of Mamutica's plateau, hoping the king waves might deliver Kajfeš and give him a chance to fulfill the promises he made during that pink tropical sunset on the remote island in the exotic archipelago of Mamutica. But that, of course, never happened.

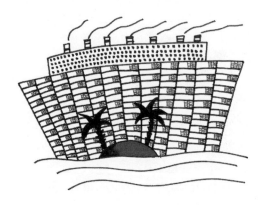

Ex-Pioneers

"HOW MUCH LONGER, Papa Smurf?" the enervated Barbies, Ana M.'s Ken, and Borna's Skipper periodically asked.

"A lot longer!" replied the visibly irritated Kajfeš, who until then, like a wise shepherd (and very much unlike a papal figure), had been patiently guiding the flock of Barbies across the sunbathed slopes of piled dirt. After a few rainy late-autumn days, the sun was shining again, luring us to the rutted no-man's-land between Sloboština and Sopot, despite the fact that the risk of emergency alerts was, well, considerable. That network of mounds and unbeaten trails and paths was our favorite natural habitat outside civilization. That area, unmarked by raised sewage vents, also served as the choice meeting place for all the other neighborhood kids, whose paths interwove with ours as though we were in an anthill of cosmic proportions. Kajfeš was at the fore of a small column of hikers climbing up to Japetić (Barbie edition) on that sunlit day when it seemed like the war had finally ended. Except the war was ongoing, only keeping a low profile in these parts of Our Beautiful Homeland.

On that grueling ascent, everyone strove desperately to keep up with Kajfeš, who, incidentally, was the only one appropriately dressed (in pants and hiking boots) and (roughly speaking) in shape. The other Barbies (in nightgowns and high heels), Ana M.'s Ken (read: a dandy), and Borna's Skipper lagged behind Kajfeš as he yodeled along his merry way. The inadequate gear of the other mountaineering club members substantially hampered their attempt to reach the summit, from which dirt provoked by sudden Barbie avalanches came tumbling down. (Luckily, I had on my Converse All Stars and not the sexy red clogs of Papa Smurf, for which I unsuccessfully blackmailed my mother in every possible way I could think of in the hope she would buy them for me.) When Kajfeš unexpectedly exclaimed, "Lunchtime!" the sun's rays

       MAŠA KOLANOVIĆ

shined even brighter and the exhausted hikers collapsed, mere centimeters away from the mountaintop. Like in the old days, everyone gathered in a circle and partook of a small rubber roast from a little off-brand housewives set, while the rest of no-man's-land swarmed with players of tag, hide-and-seek, Crvena Marica (or red light, green light), and cops and robbers, along with a few suspicious hikers. Our elevated position afforded a view of the other mounds that shook with avalanches of their own and were, moreover, inundated with all sorts of trash. From a distance, they resembled the burned Smurf villages of brotherhood and unity.

"The sun's beating down, and it's like the day was *made* for the beach!" Sanjica's Barbie reflected.

"Yeah, and we're stuck climbing hills!" added Ana M.'s Ken, shooting Kajfeš a fiery look. Although they had officially reconciled, and had even buddied up on numerous occasions, the antagonism between the two males was, in fact, never fully resolved. Kajfeš's ego couldn't bear the loss of Dea's Barbie to the arms of another, and Ana M.'s Ken was filled with the sweet pleasure of being the head honcho. Between the two men, Dea's Barbie played a dirty game, acting the part of a coquettish Smurfette and keeping the financially thriving Ken to herself while roasting the penniless Kajfeš on low heat. Ever on the verge of an incident, everything was left hanging in the balance.

"Ugh, we had *such* a wonderful time on our honeymoon, didn't we, honey bunny?" Dea's Barbie chimed in, pouring salt on Kajfeš's open wound.

"Oh, yes, sweetheart, yes!" Ana M.s' Ken replied, his voice that of a lovesick fool who subsequently showered her with kisses.

"Did you get that fabulous chocolate tan on your honeymoon?" Tea's Barbie fawned over Dea's.

"Yes! We spent the entire day at the beach. It was super great! Everywhere we went was *packed* with people! The Bahamas are so in vogue right now. Especially for honeymooners. You just lie in the sun all day every day, get yourself a cocktail, then sunbathe some more, turning over like a rotisserie chicken to make sure you get an even tan." Dea's Barbie jabbered away about doing nothing but staring at the sun, unable to organize the torrent of impressions.

MAŠA KOLANOVIĆ

"Oh, I'd love to go to the beach!" Sanjica's Barbie said with longing.

"But now we're off to the mountains 'cause there's no winter the-ere!" Borna's Skipper tuned into the lyrics of the Bijelo Dugme song in an attempt to justify the inspiration behind Kajfeš's mountaineering club.

"Oy-dada oy-da oydaoyda da da!" Kajfeš cawed back.

"Yeah, but I don't think you can compare climbing up hills and lounging on a beach—all those glistening bikinis, all that ice cream and lemonade," Ana M.'s Ken divulged, not to be forgotten.

The plural form of the word *bikini* compelled Dea's Barbie to react. "You mean, of course, *my* bikini, honey bunny?"

"Of course, pussycat! Tell me, who was the best little husband in the Bahamas?" Ana M.'s Ken slimily recovered.

"Oh, yes! If you all only knew the surprises he pulled out of the bag! For my first appearance on the beach, he bought me a Day in the Sun outfit from the Movie Star Collection. I was *so* happy…"

That day of their honeymoon was etched into Kajfeš's memory, because the moment she received this gift from Ana M.'s Ken, Kajfeš had strained to get her attention as a drowning man drifting unconscious in the turquoise shallows and showing his last jolts of life. But none of his performance had left any mark on the newly wed and sunbaked spouses.

"And when we dined on colorful shellfish in the restaurant along the beach, he asked the violinist to come specially to our table, and y'know what he played for me?"

"*California, that was her dream!*" Dea's Barbie and Ana M.'s Ken duetted, throwing in a kiss. It was a pop sensation by the band Neki to vole vruče (Some Like It Hot).

The song that simultaneously came on in Kajfeš's head was the pop deflation "Lipe cvatu, sve je isto ko i lani heeeej"—about linden trees being in bloom and everything returning to things as they used to be—but he quickly managed to regain composure, suggesting, "Heeeey guys, everyone get your cocktails—let's make a toast!"

"Super idea!" my Barbie and Ana P.'s Barbie finally chimed in.

"Oh, the wonderful cocktails we had in the Bahamas!"

"That's right, darling, 'cause you're too good for just any ole schlock."

"Cmok! Kisses!"

With that kiss, the ice pick plunged even deeper into Kajfeš's heart, a sight not overlooked by Borna's Skipper, who had been patiently waiting for her breasts to finally grow in so she could win over Kajfeš once and for all.

"Hey, lovebirds, instead of making out in those bushes, you'd be better off clinking glasses with us!" Tea's Barbie yelled and snapped a photo of the smitten couple.

"Yeah, we're already pouring drinks over here, and soon there won't be much left for you!" Kajfeš cried out.

Then Ana M.'s Ken swung Dea's Barbie up into his arms and carried her to the cocktail party. On the way he picked at a rubber roast, which made Kajfeš regret that he hadn't secretly substituted it with the gob of artificial excrement Svjetlana had gotten as part of some "Superbluff" collection. Instead, pretending everything was in perfect order, he poured everyone cocktails out of the picnic thermos—even one for Ana M.'s Ken, albeit the only cocktail he would have liked to pour him at that point in time was a Molotov cocktail. And when it came time to clink glasses, Ana M.'s Ken "accidentally" spilled the contents of his glass on Kajfeš, whose jaw dropped like a PEZ dispenser.

"That's it!" Kajfeš exclaimed, and then challenged Ana M.'s Ken to a duel.

And so, to everyone's excitement, the two Kens hastened into a duel at the edge of the cliff. First, Kajfeš fired off a slap, to which the other one responded by knocking him to the ground and kicking him in the exact spot his underwear was engraved, using his other foot to trample on his head as though he were extinguishing a cigarette butt on his face. Kajfeš then managed to bite Ana

M.'s Ken, sinking his teeth into his big toe and pulling him to the ground, after which, wrestling, they plummeted to the foot of the hill. Kajfeš was first on his feet and cowardly started running in the direction of the summit. Ana M.'s Ken darted after him. Kajfeš was getting closer and closer to the mountaintop, but Ana M.'s Ken was gaining on him. All of a sudden, a small avalanche was set in motion at the peak, and Kajfeš hung on the brink of life and death, clinging to his only salvation, a lone blade of grass—with his mauled hand no less. Ana M.'s Ken showed no mercy whatsoever, endeavoring with all his weight to pull down Kajfeš by the leg. But at that very moment, it was revealed that the avalanche had been faked. Kajfeš himself had precipitated it. In fact, he had been waiting all this time for Ana M.'s Ken to get close enough so he could kick him in the noggin at just the right angle. The blow landed precisely where it needed to—Ana M.'s Ken's head flew off and rolled all the way to the foot of the hill. It was an absolute triumph for Kajfeš, who had single-handedly managed to prove that fake Kens weren't necessarily the "little pussies" many thought they were, so he belted out in euphoria:

Mislili su neki, već nas neće biti,
Ni veselje svoje nisu znali kriti,
Raselit nas triba da nas manje ima,
Nisu tu ni bili, tad će reći svima

Some thought we'd already be done for,
They couldn't hide their joy anymore,
They scattered us to shatter us, and one day,
They'll say we were never here anyway

Dea's Barbie almost fainted and got remarried (this time, to Kajfeš), but Ana M. quickly performed a surgical procedure, mounting her Ken's head in record time. Meanwhile, a widespread hunt for Kajfeš ensued, involving everyone under the sun. With the last of his strength, Kajfeš scrambled up the mountain, and just when he was about to summit, Svjetlana suddenly turned to us with her index finger pointed to the other side of the mound and her other index finger pressed against her lips as she dramatically whispered, "Pssssssst!" At her signal, the chase came to a standstill. We crawled quietly to the top of the mound and tuned our ears to the sounds on the other side, while only Kajfeš, like a periscope, had a visual of what was happening there. When we grew completely still, we could clearly make out the vaguely familiar voices coming from the other side of the hill.

"You insane? My old lady'd find it!"

"Then what're we gonna do with it?"

"I don't know, but I'm not taking that home! My parents would for sure throw that out! I barely rescued it as it is!"

"How 'bout you take it? Your folks are alright."

"Yeah, but my old lady throws out everything that isn't essential—with no regard to whether it has anything to do with Pioneers, Partisans, or Smurfs!"

"Okay, okay. But we've got to hide it somewhere—one day it's going to be worth some serious cash."

"Well, I can find a way to squeeze the badges under my bed, but that red scarf and the blue cap and all these books—no way."

"Okay, now let's see what you have in there."

Suddenly a hubbub erupted on the other side, which we used as an opportunity to resituate ourselves and pop our heads up to sneak a peek at the secret treasures being mulled over by those older boys, whom we identified as Janko Botić, of the class formerly called "8c" (or, eighth grade cohort c), and Silvijo Kovač and Zoran Fištrek, of the now former "8d" And when we peered over the side, it was definitely a sight to see! We were attending incognito a secret meeting of ex-Pioneers deliberating the fate of all their belongings from the previous regime.

"Hey, easy with that! One day they'll be offering millions for it!"

"But in Yugoslav dinars, ha ha—come on, show me what you have!"

We sprang out of the ground like worms and recognized all the books, the comics, the records, the cassettes, the uniforms, and the badges passing through their hands. There was *My Father Was a Partisan*, a liberation edition of *Mirko and Slavko, The Courageous Troop of Peć Pioneers, Partisans in Conversation with Pioneers, Choir at the Playground, Tito and the Resistance: A Story Collection, Partisan and Proud, Long Live Work, When Tito Was a Child* . . .

This was nothing short of expected coming from these boys, given their steadfast presence on school trips to Pioneer City, which they'd helped their teachers organize as older Pioneers. I will never forget this one sunny school-trip afternoon we spent at Pioneer City, when Janko came over to the little picnic blanket where several of us girls from the same grade were sipping our juice boxes, eating sandwiches, and partaking of all the other great treats you typically brought on school trips. It was exactly at that sun-dazzled moment when none other than the Pioneer leader himself (Janko Botić) approached us and asked for a piece of candy—which, for us first-years, was a special honor, all the more so because we had, on this particular trip, luckily brought along the best candy in the entire world: the poison-green šššš candies with fizzy interiors that burst like miniature explosions in your mouth once you'd licked through the hard shell. When we extended the bag of candy toward him, instead of taking a piece or possibly two (for his friend), he snatched the whole bag and ran off in the direction of the grove, which left us deeply disappointed in this Pioneer leader who was supposed to set an example. Now that same Janko was taking a copy of the all-too-familiar *I Am a Pioneer* booklet and leafing through it. He paused on a page and began to read the Pioneer's Oath:

Danas kada postajem pionir, dajem časnu pionirsku riječ da ću marljivo učiti i raditi, poštovati roditelje i nastavnike, i biti vjeran, iskren drug koji drži datu riječ. Da ću voljeti našu domovinu, samoupravnu socijalističku Jugoslaviju, i razvijati bratstvo i jedinstvo i ideje za koje se borio Tito. Da ću cijeniti sve ljude svijeta koji žele slobodu i mir!

Today, as I become a Pioneer, I give my Pioneer's word of honor that I shall study and work diligently, respect my parents and teachers, and be a loyal, honest comrade who keeps their word. I shall love my homeland, the self-governed socialist Yugoslavia, and spread brotherhood and unity and the principles for which comrade Tito fought. That I shall value all people the world over who want freedom and peace!

After Janko recited the Pioneer's Oath, everyone broke into laughter, and Zoran said, "It'd really be a shame if our old folks got rid of this too!"

"Know what? It might be best if we bury it around here, then when everything settles, we dig it up and that's that, peace in Bosnia!"

"Probably our best option—who knows what'd happen if we tried hiding it at any of our places again."

"Totally. Check if the coast is clear!"

The Barbies remained frozen in the middle of their pursuit of Kajfeš and sprawled on the slope of the hill like so many comatose Snow Whites and the Seven Secretaries of SKOJ (the League of Communist Youth of Yugoslavia). As for us, our legs went limp from fear and we retreated like snakes to the foot of the hill, which offered relatively safer shelter. "We," in this case, meaning everyone but Kajfeš, who remained buried in dirt at the top of the hill—and in a spot visible enough to the ex-Pioneers.

"I think we're good. Those kids with the Barbies and that faggot Borna aren't onto us, and the others are far away."

"Okay," Silvijo said, taking a small garden hoe out of his Omni-Sack (after Sport Billy) and initiating the dig.

The impacts triggered an actual avalanche this time, and from the top of the hill, joined by the clods of earth, came Kajfeš—tumbling toward the Pioneer side.

"What the fu—!"

"Hey, that belongs to those stupid little kids with the Barbies!"

The boys instantly flocked to our side and thereby uncovered our espionage operation, which was reason enough for war. A real war with clods of earth, followed by a ceasefire, then a sprint homeward as though Gargamel himself were at our heels: "I'll catch those Smurfs, even if it's the last thing I do!"

Bride of Kajfeš

IT WAS A crushing realization, but it had to come sooner or later. Kajfeš finally understood that there would be no wedding—Dea's Barbie would never become his beloved wife. And like a bona fide bachelorette (following his makeover), he set out on the search for all kinds of alternative solutions that would finally occasion the fulfillment of his dreams. A plan B of sorts. Hence it came to be that, one day, out of his clandestine medical laboratory, a real live bride emerged! It was a moment of indescribable horror, which no one could comprehend until they saw the matter at hand for themselves in black and white.

Kajfeš's bride was made of Kajfeš's own body and the head of a semicrushed fake Barbie that Svjetlana had found god knows where, leaving Kajfeš with no choice but to mount his own head on her disfigured body. Indeed, no one since the beginning of time had ever before seen a more monstrous Barbie +

Ken pair. Moreover, the couple, in the prime of their passions, exaggerated their affections for each other, shoving under everyone's noses the happiness engendered by their love. It was an all-too-horrific scene of caressing—the bride resembled a champion female bodybuilder and Kajfeš a crazed transvestite

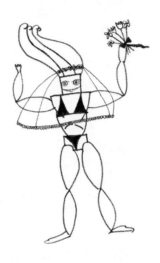

who had suffered a major accident at work. And in order to enhance this impression, Svjetlana had even smeared the newly baked bride with some kind of oil (which wasn't exactly fragrant) and sewed her a little bikini that was literally ripping off the hypermuscular body of this so-called Barbie. The anorexic bridegroom Kajfeš had, in the meantime, been admiring his bride, derived as she was from his powerful machinery, which was far from being an exemplar of cutting-edge technology and instead came closer to mirroring the scrapped-together laboratory of Professor Balthazar. And so, the two lovers decided to avenge the world for the innumerable injustices it

MAŠA KOLANOVIĆ

had brought upon them, decided to brazenly show all the other beautiful Barbies and Kens the fear and trembling invoked by their ugliness.

This collaged Adam and Eve came knocking on the doors of all the Barbies as though it were judgment day, and the inhabitants of the furnished Barbie apartments in the basement fled, to the accompaniment of the darkest shrieks, from this pair whose method of appealing for a place to rest was, after all, far from humble or modest, in the belief that deep down, people were essentially good. GRRRRRRRRRRR! and BOOOOOOOOOOO! were the sounds that replaced the doorbell's usual *ding-dong*, which would trigger the inhabitants into trying every possible way to escape with their heads. First on the visitation log was bound to be the bedchamber of Dea's Barbie and Ana M.'s Ken. Dr. Kajfeš had long awaited the moment he could finally break every single one of Ana M.s' Ken's bones, squeeze his heart dry, and gleefully drink his blood through a straw. Meanwhile, in the living room, his wraithlike Eve chased Dea's Barbie, who, staggering, tried to dial 911, desperate to save her life. But the mangled newlyweds had already cut the telephone wires, turned off the electricity, and blocked all the exits. "Don't dial the police, little girl, don't, oh, don't, dial 911." Kajfeš merrily crooned the tune by Mladen Burnać, while Dea's sobbing Barbie crawled toward the dog door at the back of the house,

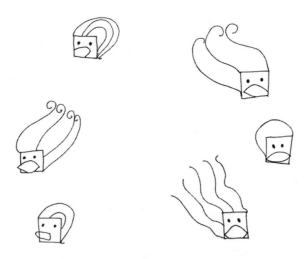

hoping to elude these Barbie specters. But all she found there was the head of her beloved Fifi nailed to the door, the blood gushing. My Barbie, like all the others, endeavored to preempt these atrocities only just beginning to unfold and wondered if they might be saved by playing dead. But Kajfeš and his bride saw right through this cheap trick, which had been retired from even the lamest horror films, let alone from children's games. And as these atrocities of unimaginable scale ravaged

MAŠA KOLANOVIĆ

that little Barbie World, the game was interrupted by the arrival of Ana P.'s brother, who descended into the basement, gasping for breath.

"Vukovar fell!" he said, while we remained frozen in our tracks, as though God himself had stopped time. *Vukovar fell.* I tried to picture that sentence. Vukovar fell, and in its place on the world map there was now only a burnt cigarette hole. Vukovar fell, and the kids there would definitely not have to attend school tomorrow. Vukovar fell, and the enemy was now closer to Zagreb. Vukovar fell, and its inhabitants were transported in Professor Balthazar's flying washing machines to a safer place.

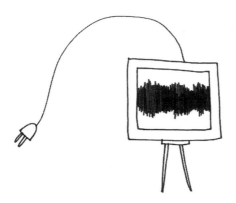

After that sentence, even our little Barbie horror show no longer made much sense. The palms we held our Barbies in were overtaken by weakness, our stomachs by needles. We split up, with some staying in the basement and others heading home. I found my mother, father, and brother looking at the television screen with an expression of horror and appearing as frozen as we had been down in the basement during that godly second which had clearly, following a slight delay, struck them now. The cathode ray tube, through a series of small dots, emitted the fall of Vukovar. People in columns were on the move. The children were crying, and all around them there were corpses—of a grandmother, of a man without shoes, of a man without a head, of a cow, a horse, a pig. Vukovar fell. It looked cold over there in Vukovar, because some of the people were wrapped in blankets. The enemy army seemed especially powerful compared to those people in the columns. Vukovar fell. There were people trying to explain something to the mighty army. Some were carrying small sacks or dragging their belongings like an ant with a reed. Vukovar fell. Soldiers in olive-green uniforms marched through the decimated town, carrying a skull flag and singing, "Bit' će mesa, bit' će mesa"—"There'll be meat, there'll be meat..."

Refugee Ball

"MASTURBATION IS A *sin!*" Sister Bernardica dictated.

We were supposed to transcribe her statements in our religious studies course notebook. "We," as in: Marina from Gospić, Marko from Slunj, Ana from Petrinje, Darija from Virovitica, Ksenija from Osijek, Dražen from Vukovar (whose father had disappeared in the fray between the Croatian army and Serb extremists), Marijana from Šibenik, and the rest of the class— which had been injected with a number of new students from war-torn areas. We were all jotting down that masturbation is a sin requiring a formal confession to the priest. Masturbation is a sin. The First Sin, the Original Sin, a Mortal Sin, the Seven Deadly Sins, Lepa Brena & The Sweet Sin Band . . . to whom my mother and father forbade me from listening when Svjetlana lent me her cassette. Appearing beside the word *sin* in the catechism was a drawing of a snake encircling a small sacred heart, which made me recall the cassette covers of the metalheads my brother worshipped. Except the heart on my brother's cassettes was bleeding, and/or suffering from stab wounds, and/or riddled with bullets, and/or surrounded by screaming skulls and gas masks, and/or crawling with insects. You could consequently deduce that the list of sins in the catechism wasn't as horrific as it initially seemed.

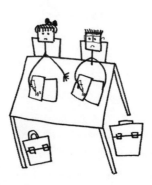

After our lesson on sin, Sister Bernardica told Ana M. and me to show some kindness to the new students, to help them study and complete their homework. She even encouraged us to spend time with them after school. The idea of meeting with them after school was hard to digest, but we had to obey Sister Bernardica. We thought we could survive extending a one-off invitation for them to join us in the basement, but we wanted under no circumstances to risk making a routine of it. A single invitation could certainly lead to many subsequent self-invitations, and then our gameplay in the basement would never be the same again. All of this worried us half to death, which was how we came to the decision, during our long break, to consult Dea and Tea.

"Sister told us we have to play with the refugees!"

"We won't play with the refugees!"

"But Sister said!"

"You're lying!"

"Pioneer's honor!"

"Well, I don't care what Sister said. Ana Cekin smells like bacon!"

"Well, aren't *you* naive—it's because her mom cooks beans for the guardsmen!"

"Well, I don't care that her mom cooks beans!"

"Beans for the guardsmen, you idiot!"

"We can play, but only *once*, with Marina and Darija, since they have Barbies and stuff, and that'll be that!"

But how were we to tell Sister Bernardica that we would only play with Marina and Darija because they "have Barbies and stuff"? This predicament worried those of us who held ourselves up to her authority and her lessons on sin. Ana M. said she could lend her Skipper to Ksenija, and then we could host a Barbie refugee ball, which seemed like a splendid idea that also agreed with Dea and Tea, and consequently with everyone else, so once school was out, preparations for the gala event were immediately underway. We connected the two plastic Karlovačko beer crates on which Ms. Munjeković and Ms. Horvat usually sat in front of the building entrance, and on top of them we placed a wooden plank (no hard task to find in the basement). Around the crates we arranged broken-down cardboard boxes from the corner store, where we could kneel while our Barbies enjoyed themselves in their full splendor. From a smaller Bananko chocolates box, we

made a stage for the performances and awards ceremony. Ana M. even brought a sash for the queen of the ball. It was a little tricolor ribbon she had taken from the corner of a frame in her foyer, where Comrade Tito once stood on display until Dr. Tuđman arrived. The only change the ribbon had to undergo was to be turned upside down for the national colors of Yugoslavia to transform into those of Croatia. Lastly, a matchstick served as a small microphone, intended for the host of the ball, a role slated for Dr. Kajfeš. The preparations took no time at all, because we only had to set up the ballroom, a process that required agonizing over a mere fraction of the details involved in furnishing an entire apartment. Shortly after these initial preparations, the first refugees appeared. Earliest was the empty-handed Ksenija, followed by Marina and Darija with their Barbies. The plan was still that Ana M.

would lend Ksenija her Skipper, while Marina brought a Barbie who had escaped from the town of Gospić. It was allegedly a Ballerina Cara Barbie, but since Marina had none of the genuine Cara outfits (she claimed they had been "left behind" in Gospić), under our breath we referred to her as Unknown Origin Barbie. But Darija made up for this setback by bringing a bona fide Suburban Shopper Barbie, which was smuggled into her humanitarian aid package by a lady from Germany who worked in the refugee office. It was from this package— among feta cheese in white Tetra Pak with European stars on its label and a lapsed expiration date, some pasta, flour, and canned breakfast meat—that this little Suburban Shopper had emerged, in jeans and high heels and a bright-pink shopping cart containing all of life's bare necessities.

Although this was supposed to be a Barbie refugee ball, with the only requirement being to arrive in evening dress, Darija also brought along her shopping cart, and inside it she'd placed a second formal outfit for her Barbie to change into when the clock struck midnight. But after the girls we had invited descended into the basement, all of a sudden there appeared some uninvited guests. Here came Tamara (Class C) from Novska with a wooden peasant woman in braids and a national folklore outfit, and behind her, Ivan and Mario (Class A) from Dubrovnik with a He-Man and a Skeletor, then Marko (Class F) from Osijek with two Bauer Lego men, and Sanja (Class C) from Drniš with a bald baby. Dea and Tea were already considering packing their belongings and raising the anchor, but then Svjetlana's Kajfeš, taking on the role of the television presenter Oliver Mlakar, rushed to come up with something—considering it was Svjetlana who had told some other girls about the refugee ball, who had then told some other-other girls and some boys, who then told some other-other-other new arrivals. The problem was that the uninvited guests were unaware that it was a *Barbie* refugee ball. They thought it was just a ball for refugees.

"Dobra večer dame i gospodo, good evening ladies and gentlemans, bonsoir messieurs et mesdames," Kajfeš enthused, immediately being forgiven by everyone in attendance for wearing a blazer with grade-school gym shorts as "evening attire." And from under this glittery blazer peeked his artificial chest hair, which Svjetlana had made out of a few hairs she removed from her hairband and tangled. New to Kajfeš's look was a white stain on his scalp he'd acquired a day prior, when Svjetlana's mother was painting a

MAŠA KOLANOVIĆ

kitchen cabinet. After his introductory remarks, Kajfeš extended his greetings to those watching us on their small screens, and to Croatian emigrants tuning in via satellite. Standing in the front row of the Barbie Aid Band, his hands clasped around large imaginary headphones, he invited everyone in attendance to join him in performing "Moja domovina" (My Homeland).

"Every day you're on my mind . . ."

Borna's Skipper continued, *"I listen for news, I measure my striiiide . . ."*

Followed by two Bauer Lego men, one on either side: *"Turmoil settles in, but love stays within . . ."*

"There's only one truuuuth . . . ," Bald Baby wailed at the top of her lungs.

"Every star shines for you . . ." Dea's Barbie pushed her way through the crowd.

Then Kajfeš abruptly cut in on the performance to air a commercial for his own products, which enraged all those who hadn't yet performed, because he'd robbed them of their chance to participate in "Moja domovina." We then spent the next fifteen minutes arguing over this before finally agreeing that the event would be organized as a mix between a refugee ball, on the one hand, and Eurovision auditions, on the other, meaning everyone would get their five minutes to perform solo. Kajfeš, playing Oliver Mlakar, managed splendidly in his newfound appointment as host of the Eurovision song contest, and his first item of business was to announce the peasant woman, who . . .

"*Moj je dragi u narodnoj gardi—my sweetie's in the sentry!*" . . . took a pass on being announced before launching into song.

The audience sang in response, "*Eh-ah-eh-ah-eh-ah-eeeeeh, keeping evil out!*" and was then interrupted by Kajfeš once more.

MAŠA KOLANOVIĆ

"Her dearest may be keeping evil out, but we, ladies and gentle-mans, will *not* be keeping her onstage, because it's time for our next performers! Let's give a warm welcome to the Bauer Lego men from the war-torn farmsteads of Eastern Slavonia, who'll be singing 'Stop the War in Croatia.'"

"*Croatia is one of Europe's stars. Europe, you can stop the waaaaar. Stop the war in the name of love. Stop the war in the name of God. Stop the war in the name of children. Stop the war in Croatia…*" the Lego men duetted until Kajfeš intervened once again.

"Europe certainly can't stop the war, but *we* can stop the Bauer Lego men—our next performers are ready for us! It's He-Man and Skeletor, with choreographed combat techniques for their performance of 'Say yo to Croatia, say no to war' by Montažstroj!" Kajfeš exclaimed into his little matchstick microphone. The two Lego men's weeping and gnashing of teeth echoed through the banquet hall, at which point Kajfeš rushed to drop-kick them off the stage. When the latest performers took their positions and Kajfeš tried to cut them off (beating his own former record for shortest interval preceding interruption), Skeletor grabbed him by the lapel and warned, "Listen, buddy, don't make me stick this sickle up your ass, or you'll look like a hairy Popsicle!" Afterward, Kajfeš sought refuge in the lap of Bald Baby, who was originally called Dada. This infant of barely a month now acquired the appearance of a skinhead who, with a single swing of her hefty fist, removed He-Man and Skeletor from the stage, then gently petted Kajfeš on the head and cooed *da da* with that special look that said "wipe my butt," to which Kajfeš returned, "Kajfeš—nice to meet you!" Meanwhile, He-Man and Skeletor remained lying on the floor, but without relinquishing their plans to retaliate against this hairless King Kong and all the Bald Baby's followers who reigned supreme over the food chain. And Kajfeš naturally had to repay Dada with media attention, so he jumped straight back into his live broadcast.

"Our next guest is the bald singer Dada, who'll be performing ... Remind us, Dada, what you've put together for us? Hello, Dada, can you hear me, check one-two, one-two?" Kajfeš pretended he was speaking to Dada from a different studio rather than sitting in her lap.

"'Hvatine'(Big Cwoat) da da ...," Dada timidly uttered.

"Alright! Let's give a big, encouraging round of applause for our bald Dada, who'll be performing 'Hrvatine'!"

MAŠA KOLANOVIĆ

"*Bruvvers all in a line, a bwoody batto we wage. Fow fweedom and fow home, my one and onwy Cwoatia on the wange. Wounds don't huyt us, the twibe's voice is wising. Fwee, fwee, you eviw beasts, the Cwoats aw coming. Cwoat fweedom fightews stand up. We newuh sell out, we are Cwoatia pwoud. Yugo awmy muss know, Cwoatia's going to wo'. Wit us go saints, wit dem hell's gates. Take cawe, dada, ov mommy, home, and sissy. We stood in der pat, wit youh son an angwy Cwoat,*" Dada sang, batting the thick artificial eyelashes attached to her movable eyelids, which came down over her glassy blue eyes when she slept. And when it came time for the verse

Newuh feah,
We wiw pusuwiuh,
Wait fow us fightews an' Cwoat beauty queens

Dea's Barbie felt she was being personally summoned. An invisible doorman swung open her car door, and she swiftly emerged from the Converse All Star and onto the red carpet, which she skipped across to the Bananko stage as the evening's unannounced "Superstar" act. Even Kajfeš had no knowledge as to what Dea's Barbie had in store. As she climbed onto the stage like Vanna from Electro Team, in a dress brighter than the brightest firework, and sang the words *No more violence, for peace I raise my voice!* from the tune "Molitva za mir" (A Plea for Peace)—from the audience there came a deafening *Ra ta ta ta ta ta ta ta ta ta ta ta ta ta ta ta ta ta!*

It was He-Man and Skeletor from the former Montaž—which now went by "Pakleni stroj," or Infernal Machine—who were firing off endless rounds from their space guns. Dea's Barbie never even reached the main verse (*Zaustavite ovaj krvavi pir, naša poruka je jasna: molitvar za mir!—Stop this bloody spree, our message is clear: a plea for peace!*) because the ballroom was filled with the screams of those who soon became corpses. Lifeless Barbie bodies, two Skippers, the peasant woman (with both of her braids perforated by bullets), and two brutally murdered Lego men were all gathered round the enormous dead body of the now-headless Dada in a pink pool of diluted blood.

MAŠA KOLANOVIĆ

Only Oliver Kajfeš, by some miracle, managed to make it out alive. He was plagued by a series of useless questions: Why couldn't this bloodshed be stopped? Why couldn't everyone simply offer their pinkie finger in truce and sing: *All the same same same, no one's to blame-ame-ame, the judge is lame-ame-ame ... And what does that make me?* Torn by all these questions, in defense of bare life and in search of a better, he stowed his personal belongings in Suburban Shopper Barbie's pink shopping cart, and, alone in the refugee column, he turned his back on this Barbie apocalypse, setting out in the direction of the dark oblivion at the far end of the basement.

Detective Kajfeš

NIGHT FELL AND everything grew silent. Barbie night, of course, when really it was an early winter's afternoon in which the wan sun came through the frosted glass on the stairway landing between the second and third floors of our building. In the basement, it had gotten too cold, so we'd decided to make an exception and return to our peacetime spot. The Barbies were sound asleep while our hands, like invisible maids, straightened up their apartments, putting everything back in order, down to the smallest detail. The best time for cleaning the Barbie apartments was in the so-called nighttime, since Barbie, being Barbie, never tidied or cleaned. In her fantastic plastic world, everything had to be polished, and all she was left to do was change into a new outfit and strut into a new rendition of impassioned embrace. Not a word was spoken about our intensive work or any other expended effort. Our nail-bitten fingers replaced Borosana shoes on the night shift, while the thin plastic bodies —feet anatomically fitted for high heels, long legs topped with large breasts, enormous eyes, lush hair, flawless teeth, nose the size of a single molecule, makeup engraved—slept soundly in their beds as though slaughtered. Beauty sleep was of the essence that night, because what awaited those selfsame slaughtered-looking creatures come dawn was an exceptionally demanding day at the office we'd arranged on the second-floor landing. Barbie and everything within her sphere had to be immaculate, because Barbie was embarking on a grueling fashion week, not some ordinary workweek typical of primary school cleaner ladies. Preparations lasted longer than usual, since we had to furnish not only the apartments but also the work stations each one of us had planned well in advance. Once everything was sorted, the first workday in their new positions could finally begin.

Dea's Barbie had a studio for filming commercials. Her latest was a provocative fashion footwear campaign she called "Barbie Shoe Fetish." The models in the studio were just then assuming their positions for a scene in which Barbie, dressed as Cinderella and veiled by the darkness of night, ran, limping, with only one high heel on her delicate feet, while a fraught Ken in the background was seen picking up her other shoe from out of a puddle. The caption read: *One is quite enough.* Kajfeš, who couldn't in the wildest of dreams be mistaken for Ken, let alone a Manne-Ken, had violently barged into the studio and jumped before the camera as a model sniffing Barbie's shoe, subsequent to which he pinched his nose with an expression of disgust. However, Dea's Barbie didn't fall for this attempt to obstruct, and once everyone had finished laughing riotously, filming continued according to plan and, needless to say, with the real Ken. Ana M.'s Ken, aside from being Dea's Barbie's lawfully wedded husband and the studio's official model, also had his own business, wholesaling dietary products, such as steroids and hormones, which helped increase muscle mass by 200 percent. That burly blond knucklehead with his Robert Redford face ran his own little personal gold mine thanks to that, at best, *dubious* industry, which had become the absolute hit of the season. All he did was convert calories into muscle mass, muscle mass into calories. And that was quite enough to ensure that their marriage (annulled only in exceptional cases in the course of other scenarios in the game) would survive. Sanjica's Barbie had a shop called Filigree Jewelers, where she sold plastic jewelry made in Third World countries; Ana P.'s Barbie had a fashion agency that recruited young meat for the runway; my Day-to-Night Barbie stood in perfect harmony with her bright-pink office at the vast cosmetics company that packed all of its products in small plastic pink boxes and bottles. Only Kajfeš's office clashed to some extent with the others' glamorous professions. After his unsuccessful attempt to play a model with a foul-smelling shoe, Kajfeš finally made peace with his long-preconceived destiny to be a detective in a stuffy, dumpy office located on the outskirts of the city. While everyone else was engaged in desirable work in Barbie World—fashion, beauty, body care, and the like—Kajfeš pensively ruminated on various financial scandals and widespread familial infidelities, along with

the occasional case of car- or gumjacking, kidnapping, grade falsification, trafficking in narcotics, smoking in the school lavatory, brutal rape-murder, and other crimes that had become common in those days. In his rather unsightly office—cobbled together from a little table decorated with folk motifs from the handicrafts store, a fake office fan, and a stack of papers, newspapers, dossiers, and files—he would sit for hours with his legs outstretched on the table, which meant that his most hideous pointed-toe shoes, with an enormous buckle on each one, were on full display. He was almost always smoking a pipe and periodically taking sips from a small bottle of the world's cheapest whiskey. He never took off his small black hat or gray trench coat, and besides his engraved underwear, he rarely wore much else underneath it.

In those pensive, solitary hours, when he came close to solving all of his difficult cases, he would be roused out of his thoughts by the smell of freshly brewed coffee, delivered in a small džezva by Borna's Skipper, his secretary. Marveling at this courageous man, Borna's Skipper daily brought her boss coffee and a newspaper, striving along the way to keep the office in order, emptying the overloaded ashtrays, airing out the detective's suffocating room, and straightening up all the files, newspapers, folders, and items of essential evidence that the office fan (a plastic mixer that ran on a single battery and that Svjetlana's mother had gotten inside an Italian laundry detergent) unseldom transformed into an unchecked chaos.

After one such workday, when everything seemed to be following its usual course, Kajfeš was sitting in his office (which not infrequently also functioned as his bedroom), sifting with the last of his strength through the dossiers of suspects accused of stealing a red Ferrari from a high-ranking diplomat and vice president of the class, while also reading the evening edition of the newspaper that most people with normal lifestyles bought the following morning. The Ferrari auto-theft case was only mildly interesting to him anyway, considering both the Ferrari and the high-ranking official were figments of Svjetlana's imagination,

because up to that point absolutely no one had included her in this game that revolved around the world of fashion and beauty and certainly had no place for Kajfeš. Then out of his doze from under the newspaper, whose bold headlines read VUKOVAR SURROUNDED, SERB MILITARY TREACHERY, EUROPE SENDS BACK MONGRELS, MILOŠEVIĆ'S GOEBBELS AGAINST CROATS, he was startled by the loud ringing of the telephone. Kajfeš was slightly confused because Borna's Skipper, as his secretary, usually handled all the calls, but since it was very late and she was no longer in the office, he had to answer this call himself.

MAŠA KOLANOVIĆ

"Detective Kajfeš?" shrieked the hysterical voice of a woman on the other end.

"Yes, ghgh, ghegh, gh hh hh hhhhg...," came his drowsy answer, followed by a series of wheezy coughs fitting a heavy smoker on the brink of life and death.

"Detective Kajfeš?" the voice repeated, as though it had missed the proof of life coming through from the other end of the line from the one being sought.

"Hello, yes, Detective Kajfeš on the line, damn it—can you not hear?" answered the now slightly provoked but fully awake detective.

"I need to speak with you urgently, sir! It's very important!" the voice continued anxiously, satisfied that it had indeed located the person being sought. "Detective, I think my..." The despairing voice began again, "I think my husband's having an affaaaaair!" and burst into tears.

"Ma'am, please, calm down this instant! Now is not the time to wear yourself out over this. Take something to calm your nerves, get some rest, and tomorrow morning, with a clear head, come to my office, Jakuševečka Street #10, near the city dump, and we'll discuss all the facts. Come at 11:00. You're very tense at the moment, and things may not be as they seem..." With the pleasant voice of an announcer, Kajfeš calmed the agitated lady, while knowing full well that, in his line of work, cases of marital infidelity were far more common than break-ins or petty thefts—not to mention how it compared to cases of falsified midyear grades. He could no longer count how many times in the late hours of the night he'd met with a lady (and the occasional pitiful gentleman) on the verge of a nervous breakdown, mothers and working women devotedly forging ahead in their careers and in their home lives while their husbands were dallying with bimbos and, instead of providing for their family, buying their mistresses fur coats and expensive jewelry, mostly from Filigree Jewelers, which ultimately made its fortune on all those adulteries.

"How can I calm down, Detective, when I think, oooh, I thi-i-ink that my husband is having an affaaaa—" the woman choked up as her voice painfully gave way to renewed weeping, full of despair. She suddenly grew silent when the noise of a door slamming shut was heard in the background, followed by steps, and then a dull male voice—"Honey, I'm home!"—after which this desperate woman abruptly hung up.

Detective Kajfeš, accustomed to being hung up on and now more hopeful that a more interesting and tangible case awaited him, perused the newspaper to inform himself about the situation on the ground—domestically and globally. *"Sisters of Charity Hospital:* ABORTION TO BE ABOLISHED*"; "Refugees from Slunj headed for Istria:* ESCAPE FROM HELL, GENSCHER SEEKS EXPLANATION*"; "Meet the barbarians"; "The razing of the village Vaganac in Titova Korenica:* BURN—FOR BEING CRO-ATIAN! *Criminals will be punished!"* The bold black headlines in lower- and uppercase letters made him dizzy, and Kajfeš collapsed onto his desk and fell asleep as though he had been struck by a stray bullet from a Serb firearm.

The following morning, the first scene he observed through his peculiar vision—which, given that the one eye was washed out, made everything appear cloudy and mysterious—was the secretary in a tight leather miniskirt and fishnet stockings bringing the office more or less into a state of order. She lunged the small vacuum far beneath the office cabinets made of connected matchboxes with drawn-on handles, collected paper airplanes, boats, and cranes constructed from the files of long-forgotten cases. The moment the detective realized that he had fallen asleep in his office for the umpteenth time, and that it was already almost 11:00, he recognized the secretary penetrating deep into the dusty hidden corner of his office with the intention of throwing away his special (albeit long-withered) plant. That deed fully wakened Kajfeš. Witnessing what had almost happened to his treasured plant, he reacted strongly, which was somewhat unbecoming of their otherwise polite relations.

"Secretary, not that!" shouted Kajfeš.

"But, Boss, it's completely withered," Borna's Skipper reproached him, convinced of the correctness of her deed and unaware of the plant's true exceptionality.

"I said *no!*" Kajfeš sternly insisted, forcing the secretary to retreat in tears to her front office.

After she left the room, he tried to resuscitate the plant with a little water, but he knew he had, by his own hand, ruined things once again.

"This plant deserves more attention," he uttered under his breath, while his gaze fell on a small, broken mirror with his own reflection—a face covered in stubble and a washed-out eye peeking from under the brim of his hat. Truth be told, the eye suited him perfectly in the detective role, and this observation cheered him up to some extent. Shortly thereafter, he heard a knock on his door, which then flung open, revealing the knock to be merely a gesture of formality, and the suffocating shack he called an office was flooded by a wave of strong perfume not customarily detectable in those quarters.

"I'm sorry, miss, but you should have checked in with my secretary first if you wish to meet with me," Kajfeš confidently addressed her, before swiftly realizing the utter nonsense he had pronounced, since hardly anyone ever came to these premises and requested his services. He had spoken out of confusion at the sight of this gorgeous, fragrant creature who'd just entered his musty office and introduced a dazzling light and freshness.

"But, Detective, we arranged a meeting last night over the phone, and I just saw your secretary run out sobbing. Has something terrible happened?" Dea's Barbie responded in a measured, demure, seductive voice, its tone, color, and intonation not in the least reminiscent of the distressed lady from the previous night.

"Oh, that was *you*. I apologize . . . I didn't expect . . ."—*such a fucking bombshell*, Kajfeš thought, considering this cheated lady looked completely different from all the weepy, hysterical old hags dressed in a schlafrock, with curlers in their hair and enormous dark circles under their eyes, cheated on unceasingly by their husbands and periodically pummeled. This supernatural being that now stood before him had the best figure in the world: she looked like an hourglass dressed in turquoise Bermuda shorts with a cropped collared shirt of the same material, little high-heeled shoes, and a mass of jewelry instead of injuries. "Well, let's get right down to it!" Kajfeš tried to recover like a big man, though it had been years since he'd scored with the ladies. "And don't worry about my secretary; she always gets a bit dramatic when her contact lenses start agitating her." Even as he uttered this filthy lie, it crossed his mind that he really hadn't acted fair to his secretary, without whom he would be an ordinary foul-smelling pile of pipe ash and files. "So, miss, you believe your husband is having an affair—"

"No, sir, I *know* my husband is having an affair, and I would like you to catch the bastard in the act, gather solid evidence, and help me strip him of his last cent."

"I can tell you're much calmer than you were last night, which makes me very happy," Kajfeš said, trying to avoid being completely wrapped around this woman's little finger. "Tell me, since you're so sure, do you know who with, where, and how your loving husband is cheating on you?"

"With every Barbie wherever and whenever he pleases," Dea's Barbie snapped coldly.

In that instant, the sound of the telephone ringing (produced by Svjetlana) blared through the detective's office. "Yes, yes, go ahead," Kajfeš answered. "No. I'm currently working on a very important case, and I'm afraid your daughter's abduction will have to wait. I understand, but I regret that I can't help. No, no ... In this office we operate professionally, in alphabetical order, so I ask you to please ..."

This entire exchange had in fact been prearranged with the secretary; it was their little trick that involved her calling the office when the rare client turned to Kajfeš for help, and him feigning being overbooked so as not to lose even this unanticipated stray. Borna's Skipper was truly the most devoted secretary in the world, because, despite her justified sense of injury (which had nothing to do with her contact lenses), she maintained her loyalty to her boss and acted out this fake phone call. In the meantime, Dea's Barbie had picked up the newspaper from Kajfeš's desk, uninterestedly leafing through from back to front.

"Astroscope. Have you found your ideal partner? Call 0066 335228 to reveal your soulmate."

"Hot tennis—prices reduced."

"Consuming lettuce furnishes our body with chlorophyll, which accelerates food utilization and heart function. Lettuce acts as a salve for the body and combats depression, heightens mood, preserves the health of your skin, eyes, and liver, and—strange though it may sound—lengthens the life of your natural hair color."

"TODAY: Croatian Music Aid and Tomislav Ivčić: 'The world is blind. Stop the war in Croatia.' Lisinski Hall, starting at 20:00."

"Today on HTV: 'Dok nam živo srca bije'—'Whilst his living heart beats.' Actors read the poems of S. S. Kranjčević, A. G. Matoš..."
"The gang laments that / there's our government, / The heart of Gornji Grad / was struck by a rocket."

"Ivan Goran Kovačić: 'O teško je četnik biti'—'Misery is the life of a Četnik'..."

"*SHOOTING AND THIEVING: Serb army on the front in Šibenik...*"

"*SLUNJ: Cluster bombs dropped on Croats...*"

"I said no, no, and *no*. I don't *care* that twenty years have already passed since your daughter's disappearance after she was discovered smoking in the school bathroom! Goodbye!" Kajfeš hung up. "Hard to believe the kinds of people a man has to deal with in this line of work." He clicked his tongue, in the hope of rendering everything more believable. "Now, where were we? Ah yes, your husband's having an affair with every Barbie wherever and whenever he pleases, and you'd like me to gather evidence so you can sue him for all his wealth."

"Yes, that's where we left off, and that's where we'll leave it. Here is my business card—with the address where you can find me when you get the first results of your investigation. And here you'll find all the relevant information about my husband, as well as a photograph to help you identify him. Here are the addresses of his mistresses and a timetable accounting for when he meets them."

Kajfeš scrutinized the photograph and raised a nonexistent quizzical eyebrow, as though he recognized the man from somewhere.

"An actor?"

"No. He looks like Robert Redford because he was made in his likeness. And please, be quick and efficient. I want him to end up like a beggar on the street with nothing to his name—the sooner the better."

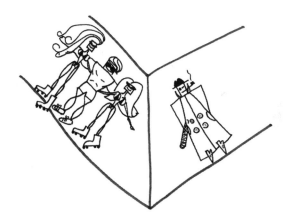

Having pronounced these words with lightning bolts flashing in her eyes, Dea's Barbie prepared to leave. Detective Kajfeš, utterly distraught by the appearance of this femme fatale who in no way resembled la misérable he had imagined her to be the previous night, escorted her to the door and said, as he threw Dea's Barbie a secretly blurred glance, "What remains unclear to me in all this is how anyone could possibly cheat on a woman like you."

"Like I said, I want you to help me leave him with nothing but the plastic on his back," she replied to this overt attempt at flirtation, with a look that sent a small thunderbolt through him.

The following day, everything in the business sector of Barbie World proceeded as usual. Dea's Barbie acted as though nothing was out of the ordinary. In her studio, a commercial was being filmed for walkie-talkies, with a costumed Barbie and Ken playing Romeo and Juliet, lovers who could have prevented the greatest romantic tragedy of all time had they possessed this exceptionally useful and practical device. After filming, she went out with her unfaithful plastic husband to dinner, in the course of which they declared their love for each other.

"I'll love you for the rest of my life, honey bunny!"

"My one and only little fig, I'll always love you and love only you. No one else will ever hold the secret little key to my heart," he said and gifted her a small diamond pendant in the shape of a heart-key that had been hidden as a surprise in a scoop of ice cream.

During this time, Sanjica's Barbie had been successfully running her costume-jewelry business (specializing in gold, diamonds, and rhinestones); Ana P.'s Barbie was preparing the competition for the world's next top model; my Barbie was considering intensifying the hypnotizing pink color of the little cosmetic boxes (a change that would, by all calculations, increase their sales by 70 percent). And Detective Kajfeš did what he usually did when on assignment—he traced the footsteps of Redford's mold. He followed him from his house to his workplace, from his workplace to his house, hiding behind the flaking red iron stair railing that left rusty crumbs on Kajfeš's trench coat. For hours, Kajfeš spied on him through his binoculars from his used Fiat Peglica, hoping to witness something suspect and enter it into evidence. For hours, Kajfeš sat at a table adjacent to his in a restaurant with a rolling tape recorder under his trench coat, hoping to catch a compromising statement.

In the process, he made sure to keep his eye professionally hidden behind newspapers with upside-down headlines that read: "ŠKABRNJA: 10 MORE CORPSES," "KARLOVAC: SENTRY MASSACRED," "Coming soon: Croatian Military Academy," "Orders to kill and raze!" "Demographers-butchers in action," "RUINING RUINS," "VINKOVCI: Everything is being destroyed," "The world hesitates too much," "Englishmen, stop washing your hands: Civilization at the stake in Croatia!" "CROATS TO THE SLAUGHTER!" "Branko Kocki-ca now a Četnik?!" "Yet another Beograd-born lie about the massacre of unarmed Serb people," "SISAK: The bloody dance doesn't stop," "THEY ARE DESTROYING EVERYTHING!" "Aca is always Aca— and always armed to the teeth!" "Forests latest victims of theft!" "CANNONS IN THE HEART OF DALMATIA!" "Included: Silvije

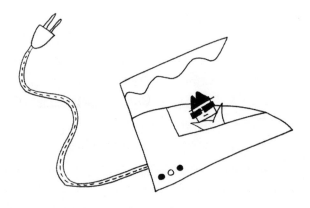

Strahimir Kranjčević's manuscript MY HOMELAND," "AIR STRIKES ON SISA"—however, Ana M.'s Ken was truly a professional adulterer, and it was quite challenging, especially given the kind of sleuth Kajfeš was, to gather the proper evidence. In parallel, the fake Redford had an indescribable feeling that he was being followed by his physician, Dr. Kajfeš, who was dressed as some incompetent detective. He sensed this plastic figurine tailing him from home to work, from work to home, to the restaurant, to the gym, while jogging, while showering... But he wasn't entirely sure. He couldn't confirm with absolute certainty whether the rusty wreck of a Fiat Peglica that always materialized behind his metallic-blue Porsche was merely a coincidence or...?

When he would suspiciously turn every which way to examine his surroundings, Kajfeš acted like a proper detective on an undercover assignment and buried himself pensively in a newspaper, pretending all this had nothing to do with the blond Ken molded after Robert Redford. In such moments, Kajfeš ended up reading past the headlines:

As the President of the Republic of Croatia and the Supreme Commander of the Armed Forces of the Republic of Croatia, I call on all citizens, and especially those capable of defending the homeland, not to abandon their ancestral hearths. History would not forgive them this. The sacrifices we must make on the altar of freedom will be blessed by God and by future generations who will not have to fight for an independent and sovereign Croatia, because we will have achieved it for them. They will be given the historical task of preserving it. Despite all the hardships and oppositions, we have successfully resurrected our Croatian nation after eight centuries and ...

Sometimes he had to interrupt his reading to order another drink as he sat at the table beside Redford's, while Redford himself read his own newspaper on the sly, endeavoring to uncover the identity of his mysterious follower:

Friar Flavijan from Ilok: Prayers likewise for the enemy. ONLY SOVEREIGN CROATIA! *Mihovil Ivanić: Feuilleton. Trenk and the brave Slavonians. The long history of Slavonia's heroism.* AGGRESSOR UNDAUNTED BY HAGUE: *Sisak under constant artillery fire! Dr. Tuđman interviewed on Hungarian television:*

The war against Croatia will be over by the end of the year. Europe's conscience will be awakened. Bata Živojinović and Boris Dvornik: Former Partisan friends, now archenemies! Inexplicable disappearance of 7 Barbies! Golgotha of Lika Croats: WE GOT OUT ONLY WITH OUR HEADS! ASPIRIN NO CURE FOR WAR!

The alleged adulterer was also caught up thinking about the headache he'd been suffering, which had become unbearable, as a result of this dizzying paranoia, and how he would now much prefer an Alka-Seltzer over a dry martini (which, incidentally, was his favorite drink). The tension between the two men, the only visible patrons in the restaurant, grew to be insufferable, and someone had to do something: flip to a new page in the newspaper, cough, pick at their teeth, spit out a bone, pay the bill.

But then Redford, without paying the bill, abruptly stormed out of the restaurant to the telephone booth, where he made a call that sent him to Sanjica's Barbie's apartment—where he was finally caught red-handed, a scene that Kajfeš photographed, naturally, while Svjetlana expertly produced the sound of a camera shutter. The very same evening, the detective called Dea's Barbie and arranged an emergency midnight meeting in his office, prior to which he indulged in a bloody steak and a shower. She arrived in a black overcoat, with a white silk scarf around her face and sunglasses, despite the hour (Barbie night). When they developed the photographs in the Chamber for the Development of Confidential Images, Dea's Barbie paid him in cash, which the detective more than deserved, and the matter at hand was completely unveiled, although from Kajfeš's perspective everything remained mysterious and cloudy. And seductive. In the background of this night that stripped all disguises, you could hear the sound of an imaginary saxophone—and quickly thereafter, Kajfeš stripped off his gray trench coat, then Dea's Barbie's black overcoat, and the two came together in a passionate embrace. Having been caught, Redford desperately tried to destroy every iota of evidence. Parallel to this present case, the bodies of his seven other mistresses were found beheaded and buried in a mass grave near the gym. Accompanying the columns of horrific news in the paper was a statement from Kajfeš: I SUSPECT THERE'S A HEAD THAT GOES WITH EACH BODY! The case went viral, and in writing, all the individual pieces fit together perfectly, regardless of how they seemed at first glance. Not long after losing his wife, his reputation, his mistresses, and all of his property, Redford was charged with the mysterious murders. His fingerprints were on all the heads, as well as the shovels they later found in the trunk of his Porsche—all uncovered by Kajfeš, the only detective in town.

And so, one evening after a far-from-conventional day at work, in the solitude of his improvised office and fanning away clouds of smoke, Kajfeš read the evening edition of the newspaper with an air of self-satisfaction. The cover displayed a large photograph of Redford's arrest, in which a group of police officers were whacking him with batons as they escorted him to a squad car, with the statement he gave between blows in bold: I DIDN'T KILL ANYONE—THOSE WERE JUST RANDOM HEADS!

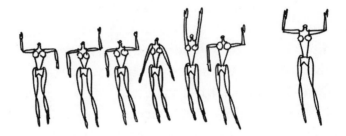

MAŠA KOLANOVIĆ

Election Season

MY MOTHER AND father were summoned to an urgent parent-teacher conference about my brother, whose homeroom teacher had by then given both verbal and written warnings that he would no longer be class president. He was caught without his school slippers and had already amassed three failing grades because he never turned in his Croatian language homework, though he unwaveringly insisted the information was fabricated and the teachers were persecuting him, citing the work of a pedagogue who once said that children, in fact, began their education as question marks and completed it as periods. His latest homework assignment, for example, required students to record their impressions of some somber war poem, and my brother wrote:

The expressionists through war thematics
Pass as though on Vespa automatics

and automatically got two failing grades for content knowledge and behavioral conduct. And while my parents were at
school for this rather unpleasant meeting, Borna's Skipper was
zipping across the rug in my room on her Vespa and chanting:
"KAJ-FEŠ! KAJ-FEŠ!"

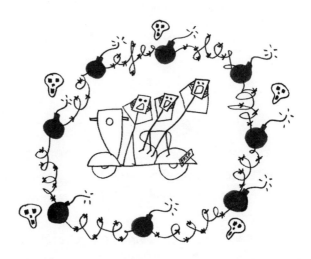

The last round of the presidential elections was in full swing,
and both Dea's Barbie and Dr. Kajfeš were running. After divorc-
ing Ana M.'s Ken (who had since become her official bodyguard),
Dea's Barbie immediately aimed for the presidency. Although
expectations were high that the majority would stand with Kajfeš, who certainly benefited from the prefix appended to his
name, the race remained tight, since Dea's Barbie still held the
ultimate advantage—she'd acquired a bona fide Presidential
Candidate Barbie! Everything happened so fast, and no one
could have expected that in the midst of the privations of Barbie
products and the general scarcity forcing the people of Croatia

to fight for everything they could get their hands on, someone in our building would get a brand-new Barbie! Aside from a specimen or two that came into our possession through humanitarian aid packages (largely courtesy of relatives abroad), getting the genuine Mattel Presidential Candidate Barbie in this situation was a real economic miracle.

But that wasn't all. Dea and her family had begun to live more comfortably and, I would even dare to say, more luxuriously. She always had pocket money for ice cream, chewing gum, chocolates, and Coca-Cola; her wardrobe was filled with genuine Benetton and Stefanel shirts, Nikes, and Reeboks; her dad had a new car; and her mom remodeled the kitchen and living room. How come Dea's father could drive a Toyota, while we still had a lousy Renault 4? Why did Dea wear Benetton and Stefanel, and I fake "Diesshel" jeans from Hrelić, the Sunday flea market? How come Dea sported Reeboks, and I "Rebox"? Why did Dea have an Adidas backpack, and I an "Adihash" one? How come Dea had an officially certified 24-karat gold ring, while mine was stamped "Made in Indonesia"?

I armed myself with "why this, why that" logic to (unsuccessfully) blackmail my parents into improving our material status, despite the fact that it was wartime and many people had literally lost the roofs over their heads. When it dawned and the sun shined down on that Presidential Candidate Barbie, our collective jealousy, an accompaniment to sheer admiration, saw no end. She arrived with her blue suit jacket with red trim over a delicate white collar, a blue knee-length skirt, and a briefcase with a discreet American flag, parading high heels and a vision of a better future. Although some immediately bowed before Mattel's latest miracle from the duty-free shop in Brežice, many of us went with our share of reservations to pay homage to the sexy new presidential candidate who still emitted the vibrant aroma of fresh plastic and whose platinum hair sparkled blindingly, as though it donned a thousand reflectors because it had just been shampooed with Pantene Pro-V. Shortly after we surrounded Dea like vultures and, to a chorus of little sighs, admired the presidential icon in her hands, Kajfeš stepped out of the dazed crowd. He wanted to enlighten the masses by giving an unsolicited speech, bringing attention to the fact that, while a genuine candidate for president was indeed in our midst, she did not necessarily have to be elected president. A murmur spread through the crowd. Sanjica's and Tea's Barbies disclosed outright that they wanted only Dea's Presidential Candidate Barbie to be president, while Borna's Skipper conceded the result didn't *have* to go that way, and we could organize presidential elections to gauge how everyone felt. The group immediately split into two camps, each with its own presidential candidate. The only undecided vote was Ana P.'s Barbie, who hesitated to join either camp because, on the one hand, she didn't really care

MAŠA KOLANOVIĆ

for Dea ever since she hadn't been invited to her last birthday party, and on the other hand, she considered Kajfeš an exceptionally disgusting figure. It was on this note that the presidential campaigns kicked off, the finale staged in our living room while my mother and father were at the parent-teacher conference. If we had a president for the newly independent and sovereign Republic of Croatia, a class president at school, a president for the housing association, a local president for the community of Sloboština . . . why would we *not* also have a Barbie president, especially since Mattel's latest invention had reminded us of the necessity of taking that step? And so began the race. Dea's Barbie ran a glamour-and-charity campaign, combining in her promotional strategies the approach of Dazzling Diamonds Barbie and Charity Ball Barbie, with mild traces of Show Parade Barbie. She organized a charity ball to aid orphaned children whose parents had been killed in the war, appearing on the red carpet in her newest Serenade in Satin evening gown, a "Symphony of Beauty and Elegance" in the form of a total glitter fest. The photographers flocked. Their flashes rent the air—"all eyes are upon her as she enters, a majestic vision in soft blue satin . . ."—while she, joined by the unglittery crowd around her, sang on playback:

Tko na tvrdoj stini svoju povist piše, tom ne može nitko prošlost da izbriše, mi smo tu odavno svi moraju znati, to je naša zemlja, tu žive Hrvati . . .

He who writes his hist'ry on hard rock, will ne'er his hist'ry have erased, Croats have been here fore'er, and fore'er on this land Croats will remain . . .

That same evening, Dea's Barbie changed into something more casual and visited refugees from the occupied parts of the country; smiled Samaritan-like at the women, children, and elderly planted on the mats in the imaginary gym; and organized a charity cocktail party for wounded soldiers, during which, out of an urgent need for disabled bodies, Kajfeš played the role of a Croatian defender. Then she organized a charity chili cook-off for pensioners and appeared in her Pink Fur collection with a

Caviar on Ice necklace, posing before journalists' flashing cameras and giving out autographs, while Kajfeš, now obliged to take on the role of a Croatian pensioner, ate a meager portion of beans made from red matchstick tops. She approached the retired Kajfeš and asked after his health, because this was how you could spot a real star from a fake. The real ones knew, under any and all circumstances, how to show kindness and courtesy to their supporters—a point she whispered to her bodyguard.

MAŠA KOLANOVIĆ

Then, dressed in a black lace dress and gold fishnet stockings, she laid an imitation Honolulu flower from her Hawaiian Barbie collection on the grave of an unnamed Croatian soldier, behind which Kajfeš, playing the role of a ghost, sang:

Bili cvitak je na spomen jednoj vječnoj ljubavi,
Za svoj narod i za tebe, morao sam umrijeti!

The white flower rests in memory of an eternal love,
I had to die for my people and for you, my dove!

Following this, she quickly jumped into her new Ferrari and sped past the war-torn areas. That same afternoon, donning a raincoat and a silk miniskirt, she visited Croatian soldiers in a trench. The Croatian defenders (more precisely, Kajfeš) greeted her with applause and jumped to her aid so her little pink heels wouldn't sink into the mire of the Croatian battlefield.

While everyone was busy admiring the beauty and elegance of Presidential Candidate Barbie, the opposing candidate, J. F. Kajfeš, took a slightly different approach to campaigning. In essence, Kajfeš built his image on the backs of speeches—speeches full of hope, idealism, and faith in the future—and hired bodyguards strictly out of formality (two fat babies acquired at the Nama department store, whom Svjetlana groomed and dressed with handsewn work overalls). Although he may not have had that Hollywood glamour *touch*, Kajfeš could boast of playing a minor role in an episode of the comedy drama *Bolji život* (Better Life). His limited capabilities barred him from guaranteeing a record-breaking economic boom or promising an automatic 50 percent increase in genuine Mattel products (as assured by Dea's Barbie), but he could pledge that the standard would slowly rise and centuries-old dreams would be realized with gradual development and improvement. His shoes were not made of gold, but rather handmade from little leather scraps that the shoemaker Šime from #15 gave us.

While his promises were more modest than glamorous, and his bodyguards hit on anything that wore even a semblance of a skirt, the only one truly absorbing his words was Borna's

Skipper. My Barbie more or less supported him because of my close friendship with Svjetlana and because of my absolute opposition to Dea's Barbie introducing a reign of terror and absolutism in the guise of a glamorous benefactor, even though my Barbie *did* secretly admire every combination she wore in her President with Style campaign. And while Kajfeš had one sincere supporter, one semisincere supporter, and two sexually active fake bodyguards, and Dea's Barbie had proper bodyguards and two ardent followers hoping a few glittery crumbs would trickle down off her table, Ana P.'s Barbie remained undecided, and no one could gather what was going through her head. Both camps tried to coax her to join their side, fanning various incentives under her nose—child allowances, clothing, medicine from humanitarian aid, and so on—but when everything was added up and subtracted, the chances were exactly fifty-fifty. The question of who would become president was left hanging over all our heads on the preelection day of silence, when Kajfeš, according to certain later allegations, forcibly had his mouth taped with a Mickey Mouse Band-Aid. Everything was eventually decided by votes cast in a small matchbox. Everyone wrote their candidate's name on a piece of paper, and Tea's Barbie rushed to take the ballot box and reveal the results in front of the news cameras before the whole Barbie World.

"The first vote goes to Presidential Candidate Barbie. The second vote goes to ... Dr. Kajfeš. The third vote goes to ... Presidential Candidate Barbie. The fourth goes to ... Dr. Kajfeš, and the decisive final vote goes to: Presidential Candidate Barbie!"

While champagne was opened in the campaign headquarters of Dea's Barbie (a celebration that definitely had to be marked with an outfit change), Kajfeš, in the throes of defeat, took Skipper's Vespa to the grave of the unnamed Croatian hero, lay down inside, and placed a Hawaiian flower for himself on the tomb.

Tropics in Flames

AS I DESCENDED into the damp and dark bowels of the building, Dea's and Tea's Barbies were already sipping their second cocktails on the loungers of Club Barutana in the Tropics. Despite her busy schedule, Dea's Barbie was obliged, as president and now divorcée, to find time for recreation and relaxation alongside the rusty old sink that served as a not-quite-turquoise Barbie pool. In this particular instance, Svjetlana was preparing the undestined-for-president Kajfeš to leave his rented studio apartment (set up on a sled).

Winter had already made headway in our parts, and the basement was freezing. Holding on to Barbie's bare legs with our hands was like holding the icicles we broke off from under the car and sucked, unless they were solid black from the exhaust. So, beside our rusted pool, we had a small electric heater named Tropics that blew warm air and turned from side to side. Apart from being used for heating, Tropics offered the effect of hair fluttering in the breeze—which Dea's and Tea's Barbies used bountifully on this particular day. Both Barbies were sporting new sunglasses, new bikinis that revealed more than they veiled, and heels that left the Barbies' carefully painted toenails uncovered.

"Ah, if only all men were like Kajfeš . . ."

"Oh, that'd be perfect—when you get tired of him, just toss him into a shoebox!"

Although he could hear everything, Kajfeš wasn't overly perturbed. He knew, in the event these Holy-day Sister–villains arranged a small funeral for him without his knowledge, pulling him through the basement by a rope in a small coffin made from a Borovo box and displaying his first-class corpse like the body of a Croatian soldier on a bier, he could always be resurrected, pretending to be Super Sport Ken or Super Dance Ken or even New Good-Lookin' Talkin' Ken. Besides, he was thoroughly convinced they would follow through with this plan so they could dress themselves in the gold-and-black clothing combinations of merry widow Barbies. And so, uninvited, he barged in on their little gossip fest—completely and utterly naked (assuming his engraved underpants technically fell under nudity). Dea's Barbie spit out her fancy-schmancy cocktail, while Kajfeš introduced himself as an UNPROFOR peacekeeper who posed for *Vogue* in his spare time.

"Are all pussies in Croatia so pretty?" he interjected as they measured him in shock behind their dark sunglasses, while Tropics ruffled their hair. His one healthy eye immediately caught sight of all the new items surrounding them: a range of sunbathing products, plastic bracelets, tiny earrings and necklaces, a pink necessities bag with a little comb and mirror, lounge chairs, and a little table with newspapers for resting their long legs. Most important of all, everything was genuine Mattel, which could not go unnoticed against the rusty ambience of Club Barutana and in the presence of Kajfeš.

"Beat it, perv!" the Barbies simultaneously fired off at him, suggesting that their new possessions had given them even more cause for arrogant behavior. But as far as Kajfeš was concerned, this merely represented grounds for an (unsuccessful) attempt at war rape, following which he performed his moonwalk dance, singing, "Beat it!" Because that was what Kajfeš, with his fake-plastic dark complexion, truly was: the Michael Jackson of this small underground world, stuck somewhere in the process of becoming White. Neither here nor there, neither White nor Black, just like the mixed halves of Kinder Lada. Dea and Tea then demonstratively thought about leaving the game and surrendering Kajfeš to the jaws of their personal bodyguards, but when Kajfeš threatened that he would, with a small hand grenade, kill not only himself but all of them, they retreated. Precisely at this delicate instant, my Barbie strolled into Barutana for some relaxation, while Kajfeš unnoticeably placed the bomb (ball of aluminum foil) into his briefcase and wistfully broke into the old classic, the anthem of all fake Kens in the fight for freedom:

Mislili su neki, već nas neće biti,
Ni veselje svoj nisu znali kriti—

Some thought we'd already be done for,
They couldn't hide their joy anymore—

Dea's and Tea's Barbies invited us all to a cocktail reception at their palace, since overexposing plastic tissue to the sun in those months in the basement Tropics posed a high risk for skin cancer, god forbid. When we arrived at their cozy burrow, there really was a sight to behold. The fact that the Croatian army had captured weapons and ammunition from the barracks of the Varaždin corps (seventy-four tanks, forty-eight armored crawlers, eighteen armored combat vehicles with antiaircraft

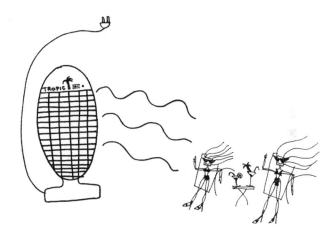

machine guns, six cannons, six Plamen mortars, four Oganj rocket launchers, eighteen 155 mm howitzers, over two hundred vehicles of various sorts, a massive amount of infantry barrels and ammunition)—and consequently became more powerful than ever—was nothing compared to the few dozen shoes, the small Barbie silverware, the gramophone and telephone, the refrigerator, the artificial flowers in expensive vases, the plastic roast encircled by a vegetable medley, the tennis racket, one skate, the mini shaving set, the purple candlestick, the artificial poodle, multiple handbags, the salon hood for Barbie perms and color treatments, and all the plastic and fantastic whatsits that awaited those who gathered at the burrow.

And there was a genuine Mattel television with the image of Barbie playing an anchorwoman for a program called *Za slobodu*. Needless to say, the top contenders on the Barbie *Billboard* Hot 100 for our building radically changed. Although Dea had increasingly more possessions with each passing day, no one could have expected such a sudden material leap. My once fairly secure status began to sink sharply, like a beach sandal that had slipped off during a swim and was now sinking irretrievably to the deep dark floor of the open sea.

"Where from?" Kajfeš asked at the top of his voice, astounded by the sheer abundance that he himself would likely never experience, even had he perished like a Croatian volunteer recruit or one of the innumerable civilians whose obituaries multiplied on a daily basis, and then been resurrected some two hundred thousand more times as Beach Fun Ken, or Here Comes the Groom Ken, or the Ken from the Barbie Army in the Middle East collection.

"We traded with the girls from #17 and picked up all their best pieces. They thought the clothing we slipped them was genuine, but it was all actually sewn by our aunt," Dea said, gently placing her Barbie on the sofa in the living room, which was the best-equipped living room in the entire history of our underground game.

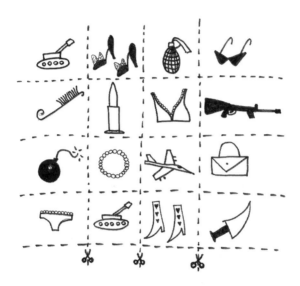

"When the girls realized the garments were homemade—after the B of the logo came off—it was already too late, because you can't get back what you give," said Tea, while from her hand hung a Barbie adorned with costume jewelry like an upside-down crucifix that dripped fake gold.

"Then Franjić's brother came looking for us and forced us to give back all the things we'd traded."

Two Barbies and one semi-Ken lay unconscious with a dull gaze directed at nothing. Only a gust from Tropics momentarily resuscitated their platinum strands and set Kajfeš's eye aquiver like a half-peeled scab.

"Franjić then took our Barbies hostage!"

"We didn't think we'd ever get them back!"

"And then Belina was passing by #17!"

"And Belina's in love with Dea!"

"Dea told him Franjić had snatched our Barbies, and Belina immediately reached into his pocket and took out a hand grenade, and he pretended to remove the pin and headed toward Franjić and the girls from #17!"

The Barbies and Kajfeš were getting colder and colder, because Tropics had stopped for a moment and began to crackle.

"It was the same bomb he used—after I talked him into it—as a threat when he stood at the window behind the school during our last math class."

"And an episode of *Santa Barbara* was just starting!"

Kajfeš was slowly beginning to show signs of life.

"Then everyone from #17 ran off, and we gathered what belonged to us ..."

Kajfeš embraced Dea's and Tea's Barbies, trying to breathe life into them by alternating inhales and exhales in rhythm with the crackling Tropics.

"Okay, okay—we also took a few other things that were never traded ..."

As soon as Dea finished uttering these words, we were suddenly caught unawares by a small explosion. Tropics was sparking embers on all sides, and the basement transformed into an upside-down towering inferno, filled with our screams and commotion. We were convinced our property would be irreparably damaged, even though no bullets, bombs, grenades, or aerial bombs had ever hit nor probably would ever hit our building. But, luck persisting in this otherwise unfortunate situation, Mr. Munjeković, who was on building watch, came down at just the right time, and with a swift gesture he unplugged the heater.

Tropics stopped sparking and the Barbies could begin returning from the rubble to their little infernal utopia. On his plastic shoulders, an ash-streaked Kajfeš rescued them from under the pile of objects, grabbing along the way the small Barbie television and a handful of costume jewelry.

Let each get theirs—who knew how much longer this war would last!

Farewell, Barbie!

WAR. HOW DID the war even end? I no longer remember exactly, but gradually the announcements about aerial threats and other dangers in Osijek, Sisak, Šibenik, Zadar, Dubrovnik, Županja, Karlovac, and other parts of Our Beautiful Homeland sailed off to the lower left corner of the television screen and never returned. And then the Croatian army began entering occupied territories. The Serb Autonomous Region of Krajina eventually disappeared from the map of the Republic of Croatia. One day, the Croatian checkerboard appeared fluttering on top of the Knin fortress, and refugees began returning to their incinerated hearths, while fresh refugees set off in another direction. For a long time, everywhere you looked, there were signs with skeleton heads accompanied by the words "BEWARE MINES!" and the cities were dotted with projectile holes and roofless houses with blackened facades, while Barbie raked in wealth from her immovable properties—Dream House, Deluxe Dream House, Country Living Home, Dream Cottage, Glamour Home,

Magical Mansion—along with her movables—the red Ferrari, Classy Corvette, white Porsche, small pink Mustang, red Jaguar, and pink Volkswagen Bug. The sirens stopped altogether, and school became unfailingly regular. For a little while longer, we continued playing in the basement, and then that too grew old. The time had come to stop playing with our Barbies in the basement, and on the raised sewage vent in front of the building, and in the little park behind the building, and on the stairwell between the second and third floors, and on the rug in my room or whoever else's, and in the no-man's-land between Sloboština and Sopot (which later became a construction site). The first to stop playing was Sanjica, who was never the game's most reliable player. She gave all her belongings to her sister, Marina, who was six years younger and naturally left out of our group of older kids. Not long after, Tea started dating a boy from class 8A, and the Barbies became *eech!* and *yuck*. Dea stuck around but ran along quick enough—with Marko Simetić from class 7C. Borna moved in with his father. Ana M.'s parents enrolled her in dance, and she no longer had time to play with us. Following Ana M.'s example, Ana P. also enrolled in dance. Barbies were no longer the alpha and omega; stories took over—about dance recitals at local organizations and schools and festivals in honor of this or that day, deed, or person. Every now and then Svjetlana and I played, but even that slowly faded. For some time yet, I hung on for dear life. With the last remnants of my strength, I fought to keep my Barbies alive while everything around me pointed to time's inevitable deluge, carrying away and scattering little armchairs, televisions, beds, boom boxes, armoires, clothing, heels, mirrors, combs . . . It wasn't easy to maintain the lifelines of all those Barbies floating away with their hollow, watery stares turned to the abyss like the tadpoles we used to collect, in the prime of our lives, from Sloboština's ponds, and store in small canteens we carried around our necks in their final moments. I played mostly in the silence of my room. And that was swiftly reduced to furnishing and decorating the Barbie apartment, both the start and end of the game. The Barbies in this albeit flawlessly set up apartment felt lonely and cold. Outside their doorstep, an entire world had disappeared, and in a flash they completely understood the horror conveyed in the picture book *Pale sam na svijetu* (Pale Alone in the World), although the criminal brood that had hatched on the *town* of Pale had been disbanded and still wandered the great wide world. I would ring Svjetlana for hours on end and beg.

"Oh, come on, pleeeease! Just a liiiittle. No one's home."

"I really don't feel like it!"

"Oh, come ooon, afterward we can go walk around the school."

"No, I don't feel like playing!"

"Oh, pleeeease. I'll buy you ice cream!"

"No! I'm grabbing colas with Tea and Dea at Moby Dick later."

"You could come over first and we can make pizza and watch music videos on MTV, then play a little and then go grab colas."

"No, no, and no!"

The more I tried, the more she resisted, and eventually she would hang up on me without an ounce of remorse. Because Barbies weren't cool anymore. Cool was Tomislav Matković from 7B, who had a Vespa and gave girls rides around the school. Cool was Darijo Natkić, who failed the grade twice and brazenly smoked in the bathroom during recess. Cool was Kezo, who blared Guns N' Roses from his room on the first floor of the building. Cool was blow-drying and hair spraying your bangs before heading to a Friday dance party. Cool was wearing Benetton jeans with a tight shirt so everyone could see the contours of our little breasts, which were just beginning to sprout.

For some time, my Barbies continued to live in that cold interior, afraid to leave the apartment, as though everything outside our little rosy shelter had been exposed to radiation. A heated debate would occasionally ensue between the sole Ken and his Sweetheart brunette spouse. She routinely caught him committing an obvious act of adultery with Tropical Barbie, but the case was never officially exposed by Detective Kajfeš. Sometimes my Tropical waited hours for her lover in the apartment, idling away the time by filing her nails or trying on every possible clothing combination, but when she finally found the perfect outfit that her darling would love, I would already be too exhausted for any talking or rolling around in bed. Everything

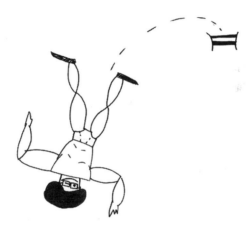

had turned into a salon-grade borefest, into some sort of Barbie version of the depressing Glembay family who often tragically went the way of Sweetheart—to Heartbreak. Barbie World was imploding, and my Barbie possessions were irrevocably drifting farther and farther from reach. Slowly I began, as I did in wartime, to embalm them and bury them in the little Smurfs suitcase that now lay under the bed along with the Vjeverica books. The box was covered in a lacy gray film of dust that I sometimes managed to reach with a vacuum, unwaveringly careful in handling this fragile and invaluable cargo. And then came the distribution phase, in which the Barbies started departing from their agelong Sloboština hearths. In the beginning I very reluctantly surrendered them to my younger cousins, but I'd simply been forced into it, and on more than one occasion.

First, I fobbed off the second-rate goods: my Day-to-Night Barbie (who had, over time, earned a pierced eye); Crystal Barbie (whose now-rickety head would, on occasion, unexpectedly topple over on her neck, as though, weighed down by fatigue, she were desperate to stay awake in the night tram with no timetable); Tropical Barbie (whose beautiful knee-length hair became a single dusty dreadlock); Aerobic Skipper (who developed a mysterious hole in her neck); and the unhappily wedded Sweetheart brunette (at the very front of the deportation list). Off they went, one by one, my Barbies, and somehow parallel with them, everyone else. After Borna, Ana P. moved out of our building, then Ana M., then Dea and Tea (each to their boyfriend's), and then my brother left on scholarship to America (and there he remains), and, like Kajfeš's eye, set aquiver like a half-peeled scab, the only people left flittering through the building were Svjetlana and I.

And Dr. Kajfeš?

Innumerable legends revolve around what ended up happening to him and where. Svjetlana had, along with all of her other small items, graciously shoved him into the arms of her cousin Marijana from Dugave. On the new sewage vent, Kajfeš no longer felt so groovy. His recognizable charm, moreover, wasn't particularly appreciated in the adjacent neighborhood. Whenever he tried to defend himself against those who were clearly better and more genuine than him, he would get one on the noggin and end up in the air like a Smurf wiseacre, landing behind the benches off Gomboševa. Eventually, he reached a corner of Marijana's room and wiled away the days, gathering dust until Marijana's mother gave him to her neighbor Elvira, who sold merchandise in Hrelić. Those Sunday market days in Hrelić amounted to a true resurrection in Kajfeš's afterlife. He found himself amidst a colorful pile with a melodica in the shape of a saxophone, a rickety compass, a broken microscope, a pillow with the Croatian coat of arms, a silent alarm clock, Comrade Tito and Partisan badges, a small piano on which a ballerina was floundering along to "Love Story," a plastic Jesus, an album filled with little Cro Army pictures, copies of Tito's speeches, a key chain with a small wooden folk shoe, a 1980s report-card booklet belonging to an unknown student who never finished his Yugoslav studies, a plastic rosary that glowed in the dark, Tito's bust, a pile of rubber Smurfs, an ashtray with the words "Our Beautiful Homeland," an *I Am a Pioneer* booklet, the damaged rails of a children's train set, *Big Ideas and Small Nations*, a billion dirty Kinder Egg figurines, moldy playing cards, clean Croatian air in an empty can, porn, more Pioneer booklets, a plastic potty, prescription glasses . . .

In that heap, Kajfeš felt significantly better than he had in the games staged by Marijana and her girlfriends. He loved the atmosphere of Hrelić, its folk music sound waves and early morning fried-sausage smells. The only part he could do without was being reburied at the close of each market day in a big black bag. In those moments, his claustrophobia became all but unbearable. Inhabiting the black bag together with all the other items was, for him, equivalent to being in one of the atrocious pits for the unidentified victims of fascism, and communism, and the Croatian War of Independence, and the war in Bosnia and Herzegovina, and all the other mass murders, and he could hardly wait for the following Sunday to be laid out again on the Hrelić turf of freedom. That was how he survived week after week, without a sliver of a chance that someone would buy him for 2 kunas (his starting price, which could be lowered still through haggling) and offer him the opportunity for the better life he'd long yearned for.

On one occasion, allegedly, he even found himself across from a pile where his attention was persistently being solicited by Dea's Barbie, who, in a sea of dirty and useless objects, lost all traces of dignity and transformed into an ordinary Balkan Barbie. But since Kajfeš had increasingly more trouble hearing and seeing, the fated encounter was destined to remain unfulfilled. And then one Sunday, Elvira had allegedly forgotten the black bag at the Žedna Deva Inn, after she got hammered on rakija with her neighbor Milan Kandža. The following day, upon recovering, they went looking for the bag, only to find smaller piles of scattered remnants.

According to one legend, on that infernal Sunday afternoon a stray dog picked up Kajfeš, and when this canine grew bored of eviscerating him, he spat him out on a meadow near the waste incineration plant, and there, sources say, he remains, among the corpses of cats and wild rabbits, living in saintly ecstasy and preaching to the ants and radioactive snowflakes.

According to another legend, Elvira's bag was collected by Clean Zagreb LLC on its way to the ever-after incinerator, and Kajfeš's body was dumped in a pile, along with empty milk cartons, a million cigarette butts, pregnancy tests, dried-out ballpoint pens, ice cream sticks, cotton swabs, tattered dishwashing sponges, blunt razors, empty containers, cardboard packaging, deodorant shells, grayed toothbrushes, wrung-out toothpaste tubes, soiled diapers, thousands of cans, millions of used condoms, billions of chewed-out globs of gum . . . According to some interpretations, he lived happily and contentedly for the rest of his life, to the extent that that was possible.

MAŠA KOLANOVIĆ is a prize-winning author and professor best known for her genre-bending works of fiction and poetry. Her books include the poetry collection *Pijavice za usamljene* (Leeches for the Lonely, 2001), the novel *Sloboština Barbie* (*Underground Barbie*, 2008), the prose poem *Jamerika* (2013), and the short story collection *Poštovani kukci i druge jezive priče* (Dear Pests and Other Creepy Stories, 2019). The latter received the 2020 EU Prize for Literature, the Pula Book Fair Audience Award, and the Vladimir Nazor Award. She is an associate professor in the Department of Croatian Studies at the University of Zagreb.

ENA SELIMOVIĆ is a Yugoslav-born writer and cofounder of Turkoslavia, a translation collective and journal. Her work has appeared in the *Periodical of the Modern Language Association*, *Words Without Borders*, *Los Angeles Review of Books*, and *World Literature Today*, among others, and has received support from the American Literary Translators Association, the American Council of Learned Societies, and the National Endowment for the Arts. She holds a PhD in comparative literature from Washington University in St. Louis.

About Sandorf Passage

SANDORF PASSAGE publishes work that creates a prismatic perspective on what it means to live in a globalized world. It is a home to writing inspired by both conflict zones and the dangers of complacency. All Sandorf Passage titles share in common how the biggest and most important ideas are best explored in the most personal and intimate of spaces.